SAXBY SMART
PRIVATE DETECTIVE

SAXBY SMART
PRIVATE DETECTIVE

The Curse
of the Ancient
Mask

SIMON CHESHIRE

Piccadilly Press • London

First published in Great Britain in 2007
by Piccadilly Press Ltd,
5 Castle Road, London NW1 8PR
www.piccadillypress.co.uk

A catalogue record for this book is available
from the British Library

ISBN-13: 978 185340 943 1 (paperback)

3 5 7 9 10 8 6 4

Printed in the UK by CPI Bookmarque, Croydon CR0 4TD
Cover design and illustration by Patrick Knowles

Mixed Sources
Product group from well-managed
forests and other controlled sources
www.fsc.org Cert no. TT-COC-002227
© 1996 Forest Stewardship Council
FSC

CASE FILE ONE:

THE CURSE OF THE ANCIENT MASK

CHAPTER ONE

MY NAME IS SAXBY SMART, and I'm a private detective. I go to St Egbert's School, my office is in the garden shed, and these are my case files. Unlike some detectives, I don't have a sidekick, so that part I'm leaving up to you – pay attention, I'll ask questions.

My full name is Saxby Doyle Christie Chandler Ellin Allan Smart. Yes, believe it or not, I'm named after all my dad's favourite crime writers. The Allan is from Edgar Allan Poe. I mean, even my dad wouldn't call his kid Poe Smart! Mind you, he called me Saxby Smart . . . (Saxby isn't a crime writer, by the way, Saxby is apparently a ye olde English name, originally pillaged from the Vikings.)

Dad is a great fan of crime fiction, and ever since I could read I've worked my way through his library of great detective stories. He has an impressive collection. It was all those stories that made me want to be a detective in the first place. I loved them just as much as he does. Which, I guess, is another reason I'm beginning my case files here: to show you that I can be just as good a sleuth as Sherlock Holmes or Miss Marple.

You might think my dad was a detective himself, but actually he's a bus driver. Not that there's anything wrong with being a bus driver. In fact, he loves being a bus driver. And I love him being a bus driver, because it means all the local bus drivers know me, and that's very useful when you're a schoolboy detective trying to get around town following clues.

What I mean is that he only *reads* detective stories. I live them.

My mum? She programs computer games for a living. She works from home and spends all day in her office, which is the cupboard under the stairs. And that's all there is to say, really.

I only mention my parents at all to let you know that I've got some. They play no part in any of my great cases, and won't be appearing much in these pages.

This is the story of my first really interesting case. Up to that point, I'd dealt with quite easy stuff: *The Adventure of the Misplaced Action Figure*, or *The Case of the Eaten Biscuits* are examples from my files which come to mind. But *The Curse of the Ancient Mask* was something altogether more

4

puzzling. What made it interesting was that I wrapped up the whole case using only a plastic bucket full of water.

It started one very hot Saturday, and I was in my Crime Headquarters. I call it my Crime HQ, but really it's a shed. In the garden of my house. It's a small garden, and a small shed, and I have to share this shed with the lawnmower and assorted other gardening-type things. I have an old desk in there, and a cabinet full of case notes and papers. Most importantly of all, I have my Thinking Chair. It's a battered old leather armchair, which used to be red but which has worn into a sort of off-brown. I sit in it, and I put my feet up on the desk, and I gaze out of the shed's perspex window at the sky, and I think. Every detective should have a Thinking Chair. I'm sure Philip Marlowe would have had things tied up in the space of a short story if only he'd had a Thinking Chair.

Anyway, on that particular very hot Saturday, I was rearranging some of my notes when there was a knock at the shed door. The painted wooden notice on the door, the one which says *Saxby Smart – Private Detective: KEEP OUT*, fell off with a clatter. I keep nailing it up, but I'm no good at that sort of thing, so it keeps falling off again.

The door was opened by a girl from my class at school, Jasmine Winchester. She was red and flustered from a long walk, and she wafted herself cool with her hands while she knocked some of the grassy mud off her shoes.

'Hi, Saxby. Sorry, this dropped off your door,' she said,

picking up the notice.

Jasmine is a very tall girl, the sort who overtakes everyone else in height at about the age of three and never lets the rest of us catch up. I'm pretty average-looking myself – average height, average fair hair, average spectacles – but Jasmine is one of those people you can always pick out of a crowd. Mostly because she's poking up out of the top of it.

'I know walking along by the riverbank looks like a shortcut,' I said, 'but it's quicker to get here if you stick to the path across the park.'

She stopped wafting and stared at me. 'How on earth did you know I'd walked along by the river?'

She looked impressed when I told her. It was a simple deduction: there was grassy mud on her shoes, she'd obviously walked some distance – because she was hot – and on a hot day, you'd only pick up mud where the ground was still damp.

'How can I help you?' I asked. I offered her my chair, and I perched on the desk (I told you there's not enough room in that shed . . .).

'Well,' she said, taking a deep breath, 'I can see why everyone at school says you're a good detective . . .'

'True.'

'. . . so I need your help to solve a mystery. My dad is cursed.'

CHAPTER
TWO

'MY DAD IS AN ENGINEER at Microspek Electronics,' she began. 'He's worked there for years. He's head of their laboratory, and he helps develop new ideas. He's normally a pretty laid back, easy-going, jokey sort of dad. But recently he's become very nervous.'

'Nervous?' I said. 'What of?'

'I know this sounds silly, but he thinks he's under some sort of bad luck curse, put on him by this antique mask he bought on a business trip a few months ago.'

'You're right, it does sound silly.'

'Yeah. But he's convinced. Ever since this mask came into the house, things have been going wrong for him at work. He's been getting into trouble with his boss.'

'Why?'

'His new ideas keep being stolen. Something must be

7

going on at his lab. He'd worked out a brilliant way of running MP3 players from your TV remote, and then a rival company, PosiSpark Inc, suddenly came up with the same thing. He'd also made a toaster which never burns bread, even if you forget it's on, and PosiSpark got hold of that idea too!'

'So there must be a spy for PosiSpark working undercover at the Microspek lab.'

'That's exactly what my dad's boss thinks. He reckons that the spy is my dad!'

'And he's not? Sorry, I have to ask,' I told her.

'No,' said Jasmine. 'Definitely not. Dad's horrified at what's going on. And so is everyone at the lab. Every last one of them has volunteered to have lie detector tests, their emails and phone records checked, even their dustbins searched! Dad's assistants are loyal to him. There's no sign whatsoever of a spy. Dad's boss still thinks Dad is the only one who could be passing such complete information to PosiSpark, and he's just waiting to find some proof! Then Dad will be fired!'

'Hmm. No wonder your dad's feeling jumpy,' I said. I would have sat back in my Thinking Chair at this point, but Jasmine was sitting on it. So I sat back on the desk and looked thoughtful instead. 'This mask. Where did he get it?'

'In Tokyo. It's an old Japanese samurai mask. He found it in a little antique shop while he was on a business trip. He buys stuff like that whenever he travels. He's not an antiques expert or anything, he just likes collecting souvenirs. The man in the shop told him there was a curse on it, but of course he thought that was nonsense. At the time. In fact, he found it amusing and pretended to scare us all!'

'But if your dad now thinks the curse is real, why doesn't he just get rid of it?'

'Ah!' said Jasmine, holding up a finger like an exclamation mark. 'That's the sneaky bit. There's Japanese writing on the back of the mask. The man in the shop translated it for him. It says that the curse remains even if you throw the mask away! The only way to lift it off yourself is to give it to another person.'

'And since your dad believes in the curse,' I said, 'he doesn't want to pass it on.'

'Exactly. He says he couldn't deliberately give someone an ancient curse!'

A possibility was coming to mind. The mask turns up, information begins to leak from the lab, PosiSpark snatch all the new ideas . . .

'Where exactly is the mask kept?' I asked. 'At his lab?'

'You're thinking of bugs, right?' said Jasmine. 'Secret agent-type cameras and such?'

'The possibility came to mind.'

'The mask is at home, in Dad's study. He works from home sometimes. The mask is nowhere near the laboratory. In any case, the lab's been scanned for bugs, listening devices, hidden cameras, you name it. There's nothing. Dad's examined the mask, and searched every inch of our whole house. He's come up with precisely zero. He's convinced it's the curse.'

'Well, it's a strange sort of curse that brings such specific bad luck,' I said. 'Must be a very intelligent and technologically-minded curse.'

'The thing is,' said Jasmine, 'there is a leak of information. My dad will get fired. Him buying that mask could just be a complete coincidence, but one way or the other, this needs to be sorted out.'

'And it will be,' I said. 'Saxby Smart is on the case!'

A Page From My Notebook

Fact: PosiSpark are getting hold of Jasmine's dad's ideas.

Fact: His laboratory is not bugged and his assistants have been completely checked.

Fact: He bought the mask in Tokyo, and now it's sitting in his study. His bad luck began when he bought the mask.

Question: How are PosiSpark getting the info?

Question: Is someone lying? Is someone covering something up? Or is everyone exactly as they appear to be?

Question: Is Jasmine right? Is the mask's arrival just a coincidence? After all, her dad simply picked it up in an antique shop. What link to his laboratory could there possibly be? Unless . . . it really IS cursed . . .

CHAPTER THREE

I HAD TO ADMIT, I wasn't feeling as confident as I sounded. Here was a genuine, serious mystery and, at first sight, a pretty baffling one. I had absolutely no firm clues, ideas or theories!

My first move might have been to check out the lab. But I decided it wasn't necessary. If all those security measures hadn't found the leak, then logically the leak was probably coming from somewhere else. Besides, I somehow doubted they'd let kids into that lab!

So I went to Jasmine's house. Or rather, I got Jasmine to invite me to her house after school. Every day.

Naturally, Jasmine's parents had no idea that Saxby Smart, schoolboy detective, was on the case. They assumed Jasmine had got a new best friend. Or else that I just kept following her home and had nowhere else to go after half past three in the afternoon.

12

As I mentioned, Jasmine was very tall, and the Winchesters, when they were all together, were like a small herd of giraffes. Jasmine's mum was exactly like Jasmine, but even taller. Her dad was so long and thin he was like one of those distorting mirrors come to life.

Their house was quite posh. My house has a flat roof and is shaped like a shoe box sat on one end. The Winchesters' house is all chimney stacks, and old-fashioned windows and interesting little bits of architecture.

'Nice to meet you, Saxby,' said Mrs Winchester. 'Excuse me, I'm just finishing something in the garden.' She lolloped away down the hall on those giraffey legs of hers. I thought she'd be in the garden pruning roses or something, but then loud clanks, bangs and sawing noises suddenly started up outside.

'She's working on a motorbike,' explained Jasmine.

'Oh!' I said. 'I wondered why she was covered in oil.'

'Yup. It's not violent gardening, it's bike maintenance,' said Jasmine, smiling. 'All the local bikers come to her to get their machines fixed. She can strip the engine of a Jujitzu T60 in twenty minutes.'

'Very impressive,' I agreed quietly, nodding wisely.

Jasmine showed me around the house. Nothing in particular caught my eye, clue-wise, but because Jasmine had said that her dad worked from home sometimes, a couple of questions occurred to me.

'You haven't had a break-in or anything recently?' I asked.

'No,' said Jasmine. 'Mum put a high-tech alarm system in a couple of years ago.'

'And have there been any workmen visiting? No, I guess your mum does all that too?'

'Right.'

Another possibility had occurred to me, but Jasmine's answers had ruled it out. It had crossed my mind that someone from PosiSpark had managed to sneak into the house, but that now seemed unlikely.

The last stop on the tour was Mr Winchester's study. I stepped in carefully, making sure I didn't disturb so much as a paper clip. It was a small room, with stripy wallpaper and a plain, brownish carpet. It contained:

- One large bookcase, overflowing with books.
- One set of shelves, displaying Mr Winchester's collection of knick-knacks from around the world (more on these in a minute!).
- One small desk, with drawers.
- One small table, holding: one coffee maker, one set of five mugs, one stack of filter papers resting on top of the coffee maker.
- One comfy office chair, behind the desk.
- Four more chairs, stacked.

Something bothered me.

'Does your dad drink a lot of coffee?' I asked.

'I don't think so,' said Jasmine, puzzled. 'Why?'

'And when he works from home, he works alone?'

'Well, yes, that's why he's got this study,' said Jasmine. 'Nobody ever comes in here, apart from him, of course.'

Suddenly, looking at the contents of the room, I made a very important discovery. From the items in the study, I could tell that Jasmine was wrong.

There was evidence here that Mr Winchester used this room as more than a private study. Not all the time, but now and again. Can you work out what he used it for?

Mr Winchester held meetings in this study. There's a coffee maker (odd in a study, for someone who doesn't drink it much), a set of mugs and extra chairs. Why would he keep these things in there unless they were used? Not used every day, because he probably wouldn't have left papers stacked on top of the coffee maker if it was used all the time, would he? And the chairs wouldn't be stacked, either.

'Your dad holds meetings in here,' I said. 'People come here regularly.'

'I never knew that,' said Jasmine. 'When does this happen?'

'During the school day, I presume,' I said. 'This makes a big difference. This establishes a link between people outside this house, and *that*!'

I pointed to the shelves above the desk. The antique mask sat among Mr Winchester's collection of items gathered on his travels.

There was a little model of the Eiffel Tower, a snow globe from New York, and a small brass plate with a curly pattern stamped into it. ('Indian?' I asked. 'Yes,' said Jasmine, 'he got it in Delhi.') The mask was propped between a carved figurine of an Ancient Egyptian god and an old china dolphin holding up a little sign which said *Souvenir of Bournemouth*.

Jasmine took the mask down from the shelf, and we took it into the living room to get a better look at it. She was

16

allowed to handle the collection, she explained, as long as she was careful.

The mask was rather beautiful. I turned it over in my hands – it was very heavy. It was carved from a single piece of wood, with holes for the eyes and a kind of grille effect over the mouth. The front was painted to give it a fierce-looking face, and painted on to the back, in red, were several vertical lines of oriental writing.

'That's the inscription that sets out the curse,' said Jasmine. 'I expect a brilliant detective like you can read exactly what it says.'

I blushed. 'Umm . . . actually, no. Not a word. But I know someone who'll be able to translate it.'

I plucked my phone from my pocket, took a few pictures of the mask – front, back, side view and so on – and sent them to my friend Izzy.

'Aarrrghhhhh!'

That was the wailing sound made by Jasmine's dad, when he walked into the living room and spotted the mask. His face went almost the same shade of grey as the smart suit he was wearing, and his tie seemed to wriggle about with shock. He picked the mask up with the very edges of the fingernails of his thumbs and forefingers, and held it out at arm's length as if it was a bomb.

'Let's put it back, shall we?' he said, shuddering. 'We don't want to upset it!'

'Oh, Daaaad!' cried Jasmine.

Mr Winchester wasn't listening. He was busy dabbing the sweat off his forehead with the end of his tie. 'The curse is bad enough as it is. We mustn't do anything to make it worse!'

'Mr Winchester?' I said politely. He paused in the doorway, in mid-step.

'Yes?' he said quietly, as if a raised voice might make the mask explode.

'How often do you hold meetings in your study?'

'Oh, about once a month,' whispered Jasmine's dad. He turned to tiptoe away, then suddenly stopped and looked at me. 'How do you know about my meetings?'

I felt like saying 'I know eeeeverything', all boggle-eyed, and waving my arms about spookily. But it would only have frightened him.

'I would guess you hold these meetings with a few people from your laboratory? From Microspek Electronics?' I asked.

'Yes,' said Mr Winchester. 'But that's a secret! I mean, what we talk about is a secret. It's not a secret that we have meetings. Excuse me, I've got a lot on my mind at the moment.'

He hurried away to put the mask back in its place.

'Does all of this tell you anything else?' said Jasmine. 'Apart from the fact that my dad's normal intelligence

18

seems to have been drained away since this curse business started.'

'It's too early to say,' I admitted.

Over the next few afternoons, I made careful notes about whatever I saw at the Winchesters' house. A lot of it turned out to be irrelevant to the case, so I won't write it all down here. But I filled several pages with information about Mr Winchester's movements between the hours of teatime and seven p.m., about Mrs Winchester's motorcycle repair activities, and about the workings of the Jujitzu T60 she was fixing that week.

I lurked in a few too many dark corners, I'm afraid. More than once, I made Mr Winchester jump out of his skin and scream when he caught sight of me lurking. But once I'd explained, using my pre-prepared cover story ('Jasmine and I are playing Hide and Seek, and I'm hiding'), and once he'd calmed down, he was OK about it.

Soon, I'd got as much information as I could from Jasmine's house. It was time to investigate further!

A Page From My Notebook

The plot was getting as thick as the custard in the school canteen. By now, I could add some more facts to my case notes:

Fact: There IS a link between the mask and the laboratory: those meetings. BUT! It's a VERY thin link! All it proves is that people from Mr Winchester's lab have SEEN the mask. Does THAT mean anything? And if it does, WHAT does it mean?

Fact: Mr Winchester isn't the only one in that household with technological knowledge. Jasmine's mum is clearly an expert in mechanics. Is that important? Could SHE be the one leaking the information to PosiSpark?

Fact: Jasmine's house is a lot posher than mine. That doesn't mean anything. It's just a fact.

CHAPTER FOUR

ISOBEL MOUSTIQUE IS ONE OF my very best friends. She's in my class at school and she's even cleverer than I am! After I texted those pictures of the mask to her, I went to see her the following day.

Izzy lives a couple of streets away from me. Her room is extremely girly, with a swirly-patterned rug on the mauve carpet, and twinkly lights fixed in a huge spiral around the ceiling. Not the sort of room you'd normally find me hanging out in.

But don't let that fool you. There's nothing pink and fluffy about Izzy herself; she gets top marks for everything at school, and she knows enough facts to fill an encyclopedia (and then still have enough facts left over to compile a really difficult quiz). Believe me, that girl is sharper than a freshly sharpened needle in a sharp needle shop!

'Saxby Smart,' she said, giving me that lopsided smile of hers. 'I got your texts. Need my help again, do you?'

'Ooooh,' I said, doing a quick roll of the eyes, my mouth set in a silly O-shape. 'I just thought you might like the chance to catch me up on this one. You know, see if you can come to the same conclusions as quickly as I did. That sort of thing.'

'Catch you up?' said Izzy, with an expression which made her look like a tiger about to pounce. Well, a friendly tiger, anyway. 'Saxby, I doubt you've come to the same conclusions about this mask as I have.'

'Ooooh, really? Here are my conclusions,' I said. 'This mask is Japanese. It is very old, it was worn by a samurai warrior. From its weight I'd say it was made of teak or a similar hardwood. Not environmentally friendly, but then they didn't have global warming in the eighteenth century, did they? And it has a Japanese inscription on the back, which goes on about a curse that will befall anyone who blah, blah, blah. I think that's about it.'

I folded my arms and grinned at her.

'Almost totally wrong,' she said. She grinned back at me, looking more tiger-like than ever.

'WHAT?' I spluttered.

Izzy had done her research. She'd checked books, she'd checked the internet, and she'd checked her vast brain for facts about masks. On the screen of her computer, she opened up the photos I'd sent her and pointed out three things:

1. The mask was made from pine, or a similar softwood, which is light in weight. You could tell this from the patterns in the wood where it had been cut to make the mask.

2. The face on the mask had nothing to do with samurai warriors. It was based on a demon found in traditional Thai theatre.

3. However, the writing on the back of the mask was indeed Japanese. It translated as 'Power plastic wobble television, blue teeth microwave paint circuit between electric lamp.'

For a second or two I stood there, on Izzy's curly-patterned rug, completely silent. I was very embarrassed.

'WHAT?' I repeated.

'It all checks out,' said Izzy. 'That mask is a fake. I think it's nothing more than a cheaply-made souvenir. It looks like Jasmine's dad simply got duped into buying a rather badly-done imitation. It's not even very old. You wouldn't find the Japanese characters for "television" or "plastic" painted on a genuine antique, would you?'

Unexpected as Izzy's findings were, there was no disputing them. Izzy is never wrong.

'Your info is as vital as ever, Iz,' I said sadly.

'Where does this leave your investigation?' Izzy asked.

'I'm not sure,' I told her.

I gave her a cheery wave. She went back to her books. I went back to my shed. I sat in my Thinking Chair, propped my feet up on my desk, and fixed my face into the special detective-type expression I'd been practising in the bathroom mirror: eyes narrowed, one eyebrow raised, everything else showing steely determination.

I thought about Izzy's first point. The one about the mask being made of a soft wood, like pine. How could I have got that so wrong?

And then it struck me! There was a clear difference between what I had thought, based on handling the mask, and what Izzy could tell, by looking at the photos of it. And this difference meant something very important! Something about how the mask was constructed!

The mask had to be made of something else, in addition to the wood. To me, it felt quite heavy, remember? But Izzy made it clear that the wood it was made from should have been quite light in weight. So the mask *must* have been made of something else *as well*. Something out of sight!

This was getting interesting! I thought about Izzy's second point, the one about the mask having nothing to do with samurai warriors. It would be very strange for a Japanese souvenir, bought in Japan, to have got a detail like that wrong. After all, if I went on a day trip down to London, souvenirs of the place wouldn't include the Statue of Liberty, or the Leaning Tower of Pisa! No matter who had made them, or where they'd been made, they'd include Big Ben, the London Eye and so on and so on.

Which made we wonder: Was it *just* a cheap, touristy souvenir after all?

And this made me think about Izzy's third point, the one about the writing on the back of the mask.

Immediately, another important deduction snapped into place! I checked my notebook, and Izzy's translation. There was something staring at me from the words of that painted inscription about *who* had made the mask.

Whoever made the mask *could not speak Japanese*. That inscription was not a curse. Well, obviously. But it wasn't anything – it was a load of nonsense! The person who painted those Japanese characters on to the mask clearly had no idea what they meant!

And *then*, another important deduction followed on from that! I almost fell off my Thinking Chair, I was so impressed with my own cleverness.

Let's take a close look at that nonsense-writing. It said: 'Power plastic wobble television, blue teeth microwave paint circuit between electric lamp.'

Now, whoever painted those words – this person who couldn't speak Japanese – must have copied those characters from *somewhere*. They *were* actual Japanese characters, they'd simply been put together to form a load of rubbish.

So! There was something hugely significant in the words *themselves*. There was a clear connection here between the mask, whoever made it, and Mr Winchester's troubles at Microspek Electronics. For the first time, looking at the words used in that inscription, I could establish that the arrival of the mask *did* seem to be linked to Mr Winchester's work. How?

Most of the words used were connected with *electronics* – Mr Winchester's work! Terms like 'television', 'microwave', 'power' and 'electric lamp' were words you might expect to crop up when writing about electronics.

I sat in my Thinking Chair, brain zipping along faster than a bike with no brakes on a very steep hill. This case was coming together!

OK, so whoever painted that inscription – this person who couldn't speak Japanese – copied the words from something *written* in Japanese, that was *probably* all about electronics.

This was what we detectives would call 'circumstantial evidence'. It wasn't actual *proof*.

Here's an example: Proof is when you have a photo of that low-down rat-of-the-classroom Harry Lovecraft stealing your pencil case, and you have three witnesses who saw that low-down rat Harry Lovecraft steal your pencil case. That's proof. In a case like that, there's no way that low-down rat Harry Lovecraft could wriggle out of it, or pretend it wasn't him. You'd have proof.

Anyway, what I'd been able to deduce about the mask was not proof. The mask *could* still have been an el cheapo touristy souvenir. But it didn't seem *likely*. The writing on the mask *could* simply have been copied from the instruction manual of someone's new camcorder. But it didn't seem *likely*, not when you add all the other clue-type ingredients into the cooking pot. The mask was very fishy. Fishier than a fish shop that's just had a fresh delivery of fish!

The next morning, at school, Jasmine hurried over to me. She looked very worried.

'Saxby!' she said. 'Have you made progress on the case?'

'Yes, some,' I replied, hoping that some was enough. It wasn't.

'My dad's in huge trouble now,' said Jasmine. 'Microspek's rivals, PosiSpark, have just announced a new range of mobile phones with built-in printers. That was what my dad was working on. PosiSpark have stolen his idea again! Dad's boss went purple with rage. He's told my dad that if this leak of information isn't stopped by Friday, he's being suspended from his job.'

'That's not very fair,' I said.

'Fair or not, it's happening,' said Jasmine. 'Saxby, you've got to do something, and fast!'

A Page From My Notebook

Fact: The mask is a fake. It's not old, it's not even Japanese.

Question: How did it get into a souvenir shop in Tokyo? And why?

Fact: It's LIKELY (not certain, but likely) that the mask was made by someone with access to lots of stuff written about electronics (including stuff written in Japanese).

Question: Can I get to the bottom of all this by Friday?

CHAPTER FIVE

FOR A COUPLE OF DAYS, things at school kept me away from my shed and my Thinking Chair. Our class had to prepare a set of science demonstrations for Parents' Evening, and I and my other best friend, Muddy Whitehouse, got stuck with doing stuff about levers and pulleys. He's brilliant at that sort of thing, but I can't tell a fulcrum from a plate of spaghetti!

It was Wednesday before I could properly get back on the trail of the leaking info. Luckily, I'd been able to get some thinking done, and I'd reached some possible conclusions. These possible conclusions now needed to be backed up with some solid facts.

I emailed Izzy again. I asked her to come up with some general research on the electronics industry – newspaper clippings, background info on Microspek and PosiSpark, things like that. Anything that might have a bearing on the case. She's much better at doing that sort of thing than I am. She's very thorough – I skip stuff.

In the meantime, I returned to Jasmine's house after school. There were some more questions I needed to ask. More to the point, I needed to slim down my list of suspects. And quickly!

What was really confusing me in this case was that motive (*why* the crime happened), opportunity (*when* the crime happened) and method (*how* the crime happened) all seemed to be at odds with each other. As I walked over to Jasmine's house, flipping back and forth through my notebook, I began to realise that this mystery would not be solved without some fresh evidence turning up. You see there were a couple of BUTs here.

BUT No. 1: The only people who could be leaking the information were the Winchesters themselves, or the people at Microspek – BUT! They had no motive. Mr Winchester's boss was confident that there was no spy in the lab, remember? (Besides, it seems to me that if you're going to pay out huge wedges of cash to a spy, you might as well simply hire the people you're spying on. It would probably be cheaper.)

BUT No. 2: The only people who *did* have a motive for the leak were PosiSpark – BUT I had nothing whatsoever to tell me about their *opportunity* or *method*. Sure, the mask was highly suspicious, but what was the link between the mask and PosiSpark? It was a souvenir bought in Japan! What link could there possibly be?

I walked home, intending to go straight to my Thinking Chair.

CHAPTER SIX

As I TURNED THE CORNER into my street, Izzy was arriving with a boxful of paper.

'Here,' she said, heaving the box into my arms. 'I've printed out the info on the electronics industry you wanted.'

I stared into the box. It was full to the top, and very heavy.

'It'll take me weeks to sort through this lot,' I said sadly.

'You're telling me,' said Izzy. 'I've got three more boxes at home. I'll get my mum to bring me over with the rest in the car later. I thought you'd want to get started straight away. Seeing as you have . . .' She checked her watch. ' . . . roughly forty-eight hours before Jasmine's dad gets suspended and your reputation as a detective goes down the drain.'

There was NO WAY that was happening. I wasn't about

to let anyone else be the world's greatest schoolboy detective!

I got started at once. The stuff Izzy had got hold of could be separated into three piles: newspaper articles, sales information and trade press. The sales information was facts and figures about Microspek and PosiSpark products, that kind of thing. The trade press was news and info put together for people who worked in electronics – web forum entries, news blogs, or exciting, gripping reading such as *Electronic Monthly* magazine and *Circuit Board Bulletin*.

I gathered the piles on the desk in my shed. One by one, I went through every sheet in the box. Just as I was getting to the bottom sheet, Izzy arrived with the other three boxes. One by one, I went through every sheet in those boxes too.

Oooooh, it was so boring . . .! Most of what I read went further over my head than a rocket disappearing into space. After a couple of hours I could barely remember my name, let alone the functions of a P238 integrated circuit micro-custard pudding mango whatsit, or whatever it was.

But then I came across a very interesting newspaper clipping. I sat up straight, blinking and alert. After a quick reminder to myself of what my name was, I set it to one side, on a fourth pile, marked A-HA!

Apart from minor interruptions (for going to sleep, going to school, going to the loo and eating), I kept on digging through those boxes until eight p.m. the following night. By then, there were four items in my A-HA! pile.

Here they are. See if you can spot the clues I gathered from them. Some of the info here is not relevant to the case, but some of it is absolutely vital! There are important deductions to be made about the guilty party . . .

ITEM 1: Newspaper clipping from *The Daily Shout*, dated nine months ago.

TECHNO FIRMS FACE BLEAK FUTURE

HIGH Street spending on electronics has nose-dived.

'People only want the most useful gadgets,' said Keith Bletch, 37, of the Shopping Statistics Survey, which revealed their findings on the electronics industry today.

'Nobody wants junk that doesn't work after five minutes, or that is not eco-friendly,' he added.

Companies like Microspek, Electro-World and PosiSpark are facing a bleak future, unless they can create new products which suit today's needs.

'We're sure we'll pull through,' said Bill Plum, boss of Microspek. 'My lab team are second to none!'

ITEM 2: Print-out of www.PosiSpark.co.uk, from the *What We Do* section.

What We Do

PosiSpark Inc. is the world's most exciting and dynamic company in the field of electronics. Our products define simplicity and usefulness in the 21st century. Some examples of our brand new designs include:

✪ PosiSpark MP25 Projection Modules™:

A range of hand-held devices for a truly portable cinema experience. Load up photos, movies and TV programmes, then project them on to a blank wall like a flashlight. [Blank wall, darkened room and good eyesight required.]

✪ PosiSpark Hidden Sound Systems™:

A range of metal plates which can be built into furniture, to act as either speakers or microphones. Listen to music through your wardrobe, or talk on your mobile phone using your coffee table. [Super-long-life 'Ultra-power' PosiSpark battery pack™ with 2-year guarantee required, furniture not included.]

✪ PosiSpark Pre-Boil Kettles™:

A range of kitchen kettles which switch themselves on the moment you think about having a cup of tea. Simply wear the PosiSpark Brainwave Hat at all times, and as soon as you think about tea, the hat transmits your desire to the kettle. [Water and electricity supply required, PosiSpark Brainwave Hat™ sold separately.]

ITEM 3: Article from *Electronics Industry Today* magazine, dated eight months ago.

COMPETITION WINNERS

We've had a flood of entries for our *Me and My Interesting Collection* picture competition, so a big thank you to all twelve of you! We printed the six finalists in the last issue, and our readers' votes have now picked the winners!

First prize
(a T852R circuit board):
Miss Daphne Spottswood
Integrated Keyboards Ltd
For her photo of her office, with her enormous collection of cake tins.

Second prize
(a selection of interface cables):
Mr P L Smith
The Electrical Spare Parts Supply Co.
For his picture of himself surrounded by his collection of postcards from British seaside resorts.

> **Third prize**
> (*Electronics Industry Today* subscription):
> **Mr Kenneth Winchester**
> *Microspek Electronics*
> For his photo of his busy study at home,
> featuring his collection of knick-knacks
> from around the world.
>
> I think this fabulous competition has
> proved once and for all that the
> electronics industry is not at all boring.

ITEM 4: Print-out of the personal blog of Dr Hans Upp,
tutor in applied electronics at the University School of
Colleges.

---

http://www.blogplace.com/fascinatinglifeofdrhansupp

March 7
Arrived Tokyo for fascinating conference, 'Electronics:
Perspectives In Sales And Function'. Hotel has lost my
suitcase.

March 8

Conference begins. A lot to pack into two days! Met a number of old friends, including Daphne Spottswood, Kenneth Winchester, and the team from the labs at PosiSpark. Hardly time to talk, so much to pack in. Hotel can't find my suitcase.

March 9

Conference over-runs until late. Everyone flying home soon. Winchester frantic to find quality souvenir of Japan before flight. PosiSpark gang suggest a shop to him. Nice how business rivals can get along so well. Hotel have found and destroyed suitcase, thinking it had been abandoned.

March 10

Arrive home. Smell awful due to lack of clean clothes. Have a bath and buy new suitcase.

At eight p.m. the mystery was solved! Now I knew it all! I had worked out *exactly* what had been going on all this time. Have you?

CHAPTER
SEVEN

I PHONED JASMINE AND ASKED her to arrange a gathering in her living room after school on Friday. I told her that the mystery was solved and that her dad's job was safe.

She asked me why I couldn't just tell her all about it on the phone right now. I explained that all great detectives gather everyone together at the end to reveal the truth.

So, after school, five people assembled at the Winchesters' house: me, Jasmine, Mr Winchester, Mrs Winchester and Bill Plum, the boss at Microspek. Bill Plum was so short and round that he was having trouble sitting on the Winchesters' sofa. His head, with a face which seemed to be permanently enraged, looked like a cherry plonked on top of a sponge cake.

'What's wrong with this sofa, Winchester?' he mumbled.

Mrs Winchester was busy rubbing the oil stains off her

hands with a damp cloth. Mr Winchester simply sat with his head in his hands, looking doomed. Jasmine kept looking at me with an expression on her face that said, 'Why have you brought a bucket of water with you?'

If I'd been one of those detectives in my dad's crime novels, I would have been standing in front of a roaring log fire, while thunder and lightning stormed away outside a country mansion (because that's what they always seem to do). However, in reality, we weren't anywhere near a country mansion. So I had to stand in front of the Winchesters' unlit gas fire instead.

The bucket of water which was beside me was there for a very important reason. Meanwhile, I picked up the mask from the coffee table in front of me.

I cleared my throat noisily. Everyone fell silent.

'Hello,' I said.

Now I was standing up in front of them all, I suddenly realised I'd never actually done this before. I'd read scenes like this plenty of times, but I'd never had to *be in one* before. So, I made it up as I went along.

'I'll make one thing clear right now,' I said. 'This mask is not cursed.'

'Oh yeah?' mumbled Mr Winchester.

'This mask,' I continued, 'is not an antique, either. But it is this mask which has been leaking information to PosiSpark.'

'What?' spluttered Bill Plum. 'Are you serious?'

'I mean it,' I said. 'All the information that PosiSpark has stolen got to them through this mask.'

'Because it's cursed,' muttered Mr Winchester.

'No,' I said patiently. 'Because PosiSpark made it themselves.' I held up the cutting from *The Daily Shout*. 'We know that the electronics industry is going through hard times. New ideas are the key to success. PosiSpark would love to get their hands on Mr Winchester's brilliant ideas for Microspek. They have a clear motive for stealing them.'

I held up a pointed finger to make sure they were paying attention here. 'However! PosiSpark know they can't place bugs, or spies in the Microspek lab, without being discovered. Even this house has been checked.'

'Correct!' barked Bill Plum. 'I won't be fooled by nonsense like that!'

'Right,' I said. 'So. What can PosiSpark do?'

'Nothing!' cried Bill Plum.

'No,' I said. 'They can read *Electronics Industry Today* magazine.' I held up the article about competition winners. 'Mr Winchester likes to think that his business meetings in his study are a big secret. But in fact, the whole world knows about them.'

Now it was Mr Winchester's turn to splutter 'What?'

'You see,' I said, 'printed in *Electronics Industry Today* magazine was a picture of everything in Mr Winchester's

42

study. He sent it in as his entry in an extremely boring picture competition. A picture of his whole study – shelves, chairs, the lot. Think about it. I took one look at that study, and I deduced that those meetings took place there. The bad guys at PosiSpark could have done exactly the same. They could look at the picture, see the contents of the study, and know that Mr Winchester held meetings there.'

'And so they made that mask?' said Jasmine. 'I don't see the connection, if the mask isn't bugged.'

'Microspek was wrong. It *is* bugged, sort of,' I said. 'But not in any way you'd normally think. That's why they completely missed it. The whole mask works like a microphone.'

I held up the print-out of PosiSpark's website. 'As soon as I found out about these PosiSpark Hidden Sound Systems, it became obvious. Notice how these systems need plenty of power. If they were going to listen in on Mr Winchester's meetings, they'd need a very, very good power supply, one that would last for months, maybe even years. The mask is made of a light wood. But it's heavy. The difference? Batteries! Super-long-life "Ultra-power" PosiSpark battery packs, built inside the mask, completely undetectable unless you tear the mask apart.'

Jasmine was staring at me slightly boggle-eyed. The rest of them were staring at me slightly boggle-eyed too.

'But how did PosiSpark expect to get that mask into my

dad's study?' said Jasmine. 'He just bought it in a shop.'

'Ah, but not any shop,' I said. This time, I pointed to the print-out of Dr Hans Upp's blog. 'It was partly luck. From the magazine article, PosiSpark knew that Mr Winchester buys souvenirs when he travels, and from the photo they knew what kind of thing he liked. They knew he was going to Japan. They made the mask, and then what they needed to do was get him to buy it!'

'Couldn't they have just given it to him?' said Jasmine. 'As a present or something?'

'They could, yes,' I agreed. 'But think how suspicious *that* would look. PosiSpark give him a pressie, then PosiSpark start getting hold of his ideas. You'd spot a connection at once. No, they had to make your dad think *he* was choosing *it*, not the other way around. And this was where they had a stroke of luck. Time at the conference was very short. Mr Winchester made it clear that he wanted to go and get a souvenir quickly, before everyone had to fly home. So what do those lovely, helpful guys from PosiSpark do? They tell him where there's a nearby shop. *They* tell *him*.'

'I see,' said Jasmine, quietly, a smile spreading across her face. 'All they had to do was place the mask, bribe the shopkeeper to tell Dad all about a curse, and bingo.'

'Exactly,' I said. 'Your dad buys the mask, brings it home, starts having some bad luck, remembers the curse, normal sensible attitude to curses goes out of the window, can't make the connection with PosiSpark, and so on. You know, that might explain why the mask wasn't accurately Japanese. PosiSpark couldn't be sure they'd get it into your dad's hands on that trip. They might have had to wait for the next one, somewhere else, so they might have made the mask fairly general-looking, to fit into several possible overseas locations.'

'Makes sense,' said Jasmine, nodding.

'It makes no sense at all!' spluttered Bill Plum. 'A devious, underhand, nasty little scheme like that? The explanation's much more simple. Winchester here is selling secrets to PosiSpark! I've had enough nonsense. Winchester, you're suspended!'

'Wait!' I cried. 'What if I could prove that the mask is one giant microphone? Would that convince you? I'm going to switch it off, by dropping it into this bucket of water. If I'm wrong, then nothing will happen. If I'm right, then the batteries inside will short circuit, and there'll be a spark.'

I picked up the mask and held it over the bucket. There was absolute silence in the room. A stab of nerves hit me. IF I'm right . . .

I let the mask go. It plopped into the water. Instantly, there was a flash, a sharp cracking sound, and a smell like burnt toast.

'Ah,' said Bill Plum. 'Winchester, you're not suspended

after all. I'm going to call the police.'

'I should be quick,' I said. 'PosiSpark will have just overheard everything I said. They might start covering things up!'

Bill Plum struggled wildly to get up off the sofa, his arms and legs flapping. Mr Winchester bounded to his feet and starting skipping about like a girl, emitting squeaks of delight. He kissed Mrs Winchester, he kissed Jasmine, he kissed Bill Plum.

Mrs Winchester helped Bill Plum up on to his feet and he scrambled out of the room as fast as his tiny legs would carry him, dialing on his mobile phone. He scrubbed at his cheek where Mr Winchester had kissed him.

'Oh joy!' squeaked Mr Winchester. 'Oh I'm so relieved! Oh Saxby, you're a genius! Oh how wonderful everything is! Oh joy! Oh happiness!'

Oh good grief! Apparently, he didn't stop yattering and skipping about for two days. I think I preferred him when he believed in the curse!

Anyway, Jasmine told everyone at school the whole story on the following Monday morning, and I felt like a hero. At the end of the day, I returned to my garden shed, and my notebooks, and my Thinking Chair, and I sat for a while and thought.

Case closed.

CASE FILE TWO:

THE MARK OF THE PURPLE HOMEWORK

CHAPTER ONE

I DON'T LIKE DOGS. They're grubby, noisy, jumpy-up-and-downy animals. They walk around in fields in their bare paws and then slob out on the sofa! Yuk!

However, strange as it seems, it was a dog called Humphrey who provided the vital link in the chain of clues in a mystery I like to call *The Mark of the Purple Homework*.

Humphrey wasn't just a dog. He was a *big* dog. A huge, heavy, bloodhoundy-floppy-eared-wrinkly-skinned thing. And he had a habit of sitting right in front of the door to my shed.

He belonged to a boy in my class at school, Jeremy Sweetly, who lived just across the street from me. Jeremy absolutely adored this slobbery great lump of a dog, and to this day I have no idea why. Humphrey could do no tricks, had no doggy training of any kind, and spent most of his time sniffing around for food. The only thing he WAS good at was drooling. That dog could have been World Slobbering Champion.

On the morning of March 16, I was hurrying out to my shed to collect my notes in the case of *The Tomb of Death*. I was already running late, and would have to jog to school. And there was Humphrey, with his bum parked right in front of the shed door.

I whistled. I spoke nicely. I tugged at his collar. He wouldn't move. I yelled. I shouted. There was no way I could get the shed door open with that dopey great hound plonked there.

I went round to Jeremy's house. 'He's outside my shed again!' I cried.

'Sorry,' said Jeremy with a weak smile. 'There must be something in there he likes the smell of.'

'Isn't there any way to keep him safely in your house?'

'He keeps getting out. He likes to wander around. He's a very intelligent dog.'

'Really,' I said flatly.

Jeremy followed me back to the shed. He made one little 'tkk-tkk' noise and Humphrey lumbered to his feet (or rather his paws) and lolloped after his owner. I stepped over the puddle of drool outside my shed and collected my notes.

Jeremy Sweetly. He was a nice guy. Nicey-nice. Too nice for his own good. He was, to be brutally honest, the St Egbert's School resident wet drip. He showed no embarrassment whatsoever at admitting he carried a miniature teddy bear called Norman around with him.

Don't get me wrong, I liked him. Everybody did. He was so kind-hearted he made charity workers look like an evil villain's henchmen! But he was never exactly the first with his hand up in class – 'Oooh, me, me, I know!' – even when he knew the answer.

The basic nature of Jeremy Sweetly was to be highly significant in this case.

I was almost late for school that day. Running like mad, I nearly collided with the school caretaker's ladder on the way in (he was fixing the leaky roof over the toilets).

Jeremy was almost late too, probably because he'd spent several minutes getting Humphrey back into his house, and then several minutes more saying bye-bye-my-wikkle-doggie, etc, etc.

That day marked the official launch of this year's School Essay Challenge. Every spring term, all the local schools took part in a competition; we all wrote illustrated essays on whatever topic happened to appeal to us. There was a winner in each school (who got a twenty-pound book voucher or something like that) and the winners from each school had their essays judged by all the head teachers. The overall winner got a big prize, like a bike or a games console.

'This year's prize,' said Mrs Penzler, our form teacher, 'is a laptop computer.'

'Oooh,' said the class. All of the class except me, that is. I made a sort of wheezy noise because I was still out of breath from running to school. 'I'm so unfit!' I gasped to myself.

Mostly, everyone kept their essay subject a secret until handing-in time. I don't know why. We just did. It made for some fun gossip. But, me being a detective, I tended to work out what most people were doing for their essay within the first week.

All eyes were on Jeremy Sweetly. He was hot favourite to win this year: he'd come second two years ago, and won the overall prize last year with a very interesting piece entitled *The Life Story of My Dad*.

For a few days, the entire class spent their lunchtimes sneaking around the school library and downloading stuff in the ICT suite. I saw Jeremy a couple of times in the local records section at the library in town and talking to the people who'd lived in the house next door to the school since roughly the beginning of time. I'd decided to enter a certain case file, entitled *The Curse of the Ancient Mask*.

I swapped titles with my two friends, Izzy Moustique and George 'Muddy' Whitehouse, partly because we were best buddies and partly because there was no way Muddy would be able to keep his essay secret for long. He'd get too excited and blab.

Izzy's essay was going to be called *Global Warming and Sun/Cosmic Ray Activity* and be packed with diagrams. Muddy was doing a how-to thing about making your own self-propelling bicycle.

'Have you worked out what he's doing yet?' whispered Muddy, when we spotted Jeremy coming out of the busy Staff Room one afternoon with a bundle of notes under his arm.

'Hmm,' I said. 'Well, he's not been in the Staff Room because he's got into trouble with a teacher. Jeremy Sweetly does not get into trouble. Sooooo . . . Yes, having observed him over the past few days, I think I've got a good idea of what he's writing about.'

Have you worked it out?

'He's writing about the school,' I said. 'More probably, the history of the school. He's been looking up local records and talking to people who'd know about that.'

Muddy whistled with admiration. 'Now *that* is a real teacher-pleaser,' he said, scratching his knee and sending a little shower of dried mud to the floor.

'I think our Jeremy's going to do it again,' I said, nodding.

I was completely wrong!

The following morning, a crime came to light. Mrs Penzler gave us half an hour to work on our essays before starting the first lesson. We all reached into our school bags and pulled out our various notebooks and print-outs. Jeremy Sweetly pulled out the CD on which he'd stored all his research.

The disc was ruined! It had been coated in a thick, purple substance which had dried all hard and rubbery. Slapped in the middle of this stuff was a slip of paper, neatly cut from a magazine of some sort, on which was printed in large letters:

YOU HAVE BEEN GOT
BY THE PURPLE AVENGER!
HA! HA!

He held the CD up between thumb and forefinger, speechless with shock. At that moment, the entire class gave what would become, during this case, the first in a trilogy of loud gasps.

CHAPTER
TWO

I QUICKLY MADE A MENTAL list of suspects. The list read:

- Everyone!

The whole class had a motive. The whole *school* had a motive! We *all* knew that Jeremy Sweetly had the best chance of winning the competition. Anyone might have done it, in order to knock the favourite out of the running.

Which didn't exactly make things easy. As soon as the entire class had stopped gasping, they looked straight at me. This was clearly a case for my detective skills. (At least, I *hope* that's why they looked straight at me . . .)

'Aren't the files still on a computer, Jeremy?' asked Mrs Penzler. She hadn't gasped. Mrs Penzler was a no-nonsense sort of teacher. Whatever she wore always looked like it was standing to attention, and she had strange, pebble glasses which made her look as though she had no eyes whatsoever.

'I transferred everything off the school computer to this disc yesterday,' wailed Jeremy, 'and I was going to back it up on my home computer tonight. I never kept the hard copies of my notes. I've lost the lot!'

'Oh,' said Mrs Penzler, sadly. For Mrs Penzler, this was showing great sympathy. A sad 'oh' was her equivalent of rushing over and giving him a hug. 'You'll never have time to do it all again before the essays are due to be handed in,' she said.

Jeremy's lower lip started fluttering like a leaf in a hurricane. Meanwhile, my attention was drawn to the back of the classroom. My list of suspects might have included everyone, but there was one person who was sure to be at the top of it: that low-down rat Harry Lovecraft. Sure enough, he was sitting there, at his desk, smirking evilly to himself.

After the bell rang for break time, Muddy and I went over to Jeremy Sweetly's desk. Once we'd given him a tissue and he'd given his nose a good blow, he started to feel a bit better.

'I'm out of the competition now,' he said.

'Maybe you could scrape that stuff off the disc?' said

Muddy. 'I dropped my alarm clock down our loo by mistake once, and it still works. Mostly.'

'That's not really the same thing, Muddy,' I said. 'And how on earth did you . . .? Hmm, never mind.'

I examined the ruined disc. What *was* that purple stuff? From the way it formed a sort of gloopy shape, it had obviously been some kind of thick liquid, which had then dried to form a rubbery, slightly sticky layer. The piece of paper had been pressed into it while it was still wet. On closer inspection, the paper was from a comic strip – there was half a face and a bit of speech bubble.

'So who's The Purple Avenger?' asked Muddy.

'I'll give you one guess,' I said. I raised my voice, to make sure that low-down rat Harry Lovecraft heard me. He was passing us, on his way out of the classroom.

'Don't look at me, Smart,' he said. 'If Sweetly here can't look after his stuff, that's his own problem.'

'I saw you smirking!' I told him. 'I know you're behind this!'

'Not guilty,' said Harry. If he was any slimier, he'd have been a toad. Harry Lovecraft was the only person I'd ever met who could play football in February and not get mud on his shorts. He had shiny black hair cut in perfectly straight lines, and shiny black shoes, and weasely eyes. He had the sort of face that demanded a thin, twirly moustache, like a baddie in an old movie. The guy just oozed snottiness.

'Accidents will happen,' he said, grinning.

'Yes,' I said, 'convenient accidents that put the front runner in the competition out of the picture.'

'Oh yeeeeees,' said Harry, pretending to be surprised. 'I hadn't thought of that.'

And off he smarmed. Eurgh!

'Don't you worry, Jeremy,' I said. 'Saxby Smart is on the case! That low-down rat won't get away with it.'

'No, no, no,' said Jeremy. 'He's right. It was an accident. I don't need you to investigate anything, really.'

'Don't be daft,' said Muddy. 'That disc's been wrecked on purpose.'

'I'm sure something just tipped over into my bag. That's all. Just an unfortunate accident. Honest,' said Jeremy. 'It's probably jam. My mum probably knocked a jar over and in it all plopped. Never mind.'

I frowned. 'You don't think it was sabotage?'

'Oh, no, no.'

'Then how do you explain the note from The Purple Avenger?' I asked.

'It must have torn out of the superhero comic I was reading. Look!'

And out of his bag he produced a recent issue of a

comic book that was indeed entitled *The Purple Avenger* (*Trouble in the Skies! The Avenger Faces DOOOOOM!*). It certainly looked tatty, all ripped at the corners and wrinkly.

'Oh,' said Muddy. 'Well, perhaps it was an accident after all.'

But I was highly suspicious! From my examination of the disc, I knew that the piece of paper hadn't simply been torn out of Jeremy's comic book. How?

I knew because that paper, stuck to the disc, was neatly cut. If it had been accidentally torn from the comic book, it would have had rough edges.

'So, Jeremy,' I said. 'You're convinced it was an accident?'

'Must have been,' said Jeremy quickly. 'I put the disc in this bag yesterday, straight out of one of the computers in the ICT suite. It's never left the bag. I swear!'

'Do you mind if I peek inside the bag?' I asked.

'No problem,' said Jeremy. He emptied out the contents on to his desk. There was:

- One homework book
- Two paperbacks
- One pencil case
- One tatty Purple Avenger comic book
- One miniature teddy bear called Norman

He put them in a line, all clean and tidy (well, except the comic book!). I looked inside the bag. Empty. None of the grit and stains that seem to generally collect inside school bags!

'And the disc hasn't left the bag?' I asked. 'Not once?'

'Absolutely not,' said Jeremy.

I *knew* he was mistaken. The disc *must* have been taken out of the bag at some point.

How did I know?

The contents of the bag, and the bag itself, were clean. If that purple-something had been tipped into the bag like Jeremy thought, it would have ended up on more than just the disc. Therefore, the disc must have been removed. Which made it all the more likely that it had been deliberately ruined.

'Well, I'm so glad we've sorted all that out,' said Jeremy. 'Just my bad luck! Oh well, there's always next year.'

'Do you mind if I keep the disc?' I said.

'Not at all,' said Jeremy, handing it over. 'It's no good to anyone now.'

He gathered up his stuff and hurried away.

'So,' said Muddy, 'looks like there's no case for Saxby Smart after all.'

'On the contrary!' I said, turning the disc over and over in my hands. 'He's hiding something.'

'Oh, come on!' said Muddy. 'If he thought it was sabotage, he'd have said! The only reason he'd start covering it up was if he'd done it himself! And that's just plain maaaaad!' He made a twirling motion with his finger and pulled a loopy face.

'Hmm,' I said. 'Just plain mad . . .'

A Page From My Notebook

Fact: Jeremy Sweetly IS covering something up.

Question: WHY??? He is the only person in the school who would NOT have a motive for ruining his work!

Fact: Harry Lovecraft is a low-down rat. (BUT I must be fair at all times. So far, there's nothing to link him to the disc.)

Fact: Even if Harry Lovecraft DIDN'T do it, that still leaves a couple of hundred possible suspects . . . Including all my friends!

I must try to do three things:
1. Work out *why* Jeremy would want to lie.
2. Work out what that purple stuff is – this might be an important lead.
3. Work out if there are any other clues to be had from this disc.

CHAPTER
THREE

THERE WAS ONE FURTHER CLUE to be had from the disc. That
message from The Purple Avenger - *You have been got . . .* –
on closer examination looked like it had been printed
separately on top of the cut-out piece of comic book. If I
could trace the computer it had been printed from, that
might give me a lead.

It was a pretty thin clue, as clues go, but it was the only
one I had. I went to Izzy Moustique's house after school,
and explained the problem.

'That's a pretty thin clue, as clues go,' she said.

'I know,' I grumbled.

She took a quick scan of the disc, for her records, and
held it under the light from the pink-shaded lamp on her
flower-stickered desk.

'I doubt there'll be much info to be had from this,' she said. And when a brainbox like Izzy says something like that, you might as well give up. 'Could Saxby Smart have met his match?'

'Certainly not,' I said with a sly smile. 'Every problem has a solution.' I rubbed my chin in a particularly detectivey way. 'Why go to the trouble of creating the note? Why not just ruin the disc?'

'Exactly,' said Izzy. 'The note shows that the damage can't possibly have been accidental.'

'It's as if this Purple Avenger person is gloating,' I said. 'Ha ha, you can't catch me. By the way, have you any idea what that purple stuff is?'

'I've come up with some possibilities,' said Izzy. She picked at a bit of the stuff and it snapped off with a rubbery twang. She swung around on her brightly cushioned swivel chair and pulled a couple of print-outs across her desk.

'It's not any type of paint,' she said, running a finger down the print-out. Most of her fingers were sporting chunky rings with fake jewels today. 'And, as you say, it must have started as liquid and then set. There are three things it might be . . .'

And they were:

1. A type of heavy-duty sealant, used in DIY for making things waterproof.

2. A glue used by people who install kitchens, for sticking worktops together, that sort of thing.

3. An insulator, normally used in very small amounts inside computers, to protect the most delicate circuits.

'And would Jeremy Sweetly be likely to have a supply of any of those to hand?' said Izzy, shrugging her shoulders. 'He's not exactly into things like DIY and kitchen installation, is he?'

'No,' I said. 'You wouldn't find them in many . . . Wait!' A memory flashed across my brain. A memory from that morning, rushing to school! 'Wait!' I cried. 'I know what it might be! It *is* one of those three possibilities!'

Have you spotted it?

'It's waterproof DIY sealing thingummy whatsit!' I cried. 'The school caretaker was fixing the leaky roof this morning. I bet he used something like that.'

'So the disc was damaged at school,' said Izzy. 'Not at Jeremy's house.'

'Most probably.'

Of course, this didn't help me work out who had damaged the disc, but it gave me an important starting point. I left the disc with Izzy, thanked her for her help, and dashed home.

I needed my Thinking Chair. I went to the garden shed, plonked myself down and propped my feet up on my tiny, overcrowded desk. I stared out of the perspex window at the rapidly fading daylight, and considered things.

Jeremy said he'd run that disc off yesterday, in the school ICT suite. Assuming that was true, then the disc must have been ruined during school hours yesterday. It couldn't have been damaged this morning, because the waterproof DIY sealing thingummy whatsit had dried hard, and that would have taken a while.

So when could The Purple Avenger have struck? During lunch break? Possibly, but surely Jeremy would have noticed the disc was damaged, or at least missing, by the afternoon?

I phoned Izzy back. 'Could you get me a list of everyone

who was in school yesterday after normal hours? Apart from the staff; they'd have no motive.'

'No problem. I'll have it in the morning,' said Izzy.

Our head teacher is very keen on sticking to the rules. And Rule Number One in her rulebook is 'Nobody Is Allowed In School After Hours Without Permission'. Not so much as an ant could wander the corridors without appearing on the official lists. Which, in this case, was good news for my investigation.

I sat in my Thinking Chair until it was nearly dark. By then it was getting cold outside, and I was getting hungry, but, as I tried to leave, the door to the shed wouldn't budge. I realised Humphrey must have escaped again. I was pushing and yelling for twenty minutes before the wretched hound would move his fat behind.

A Page From My Notebook

SO! The Purple Avenger must have taken the disc from Jeremy's bag at school, covered it in waterproof DIY sealing thingummy whatsit, let it dry, then replaced the disc in the bag. **IF** Izzy's list shows that Jeremy was in school after normal hours, then THAT would seem the likely time that The Avenger struck. (Because there would be far fewer people around after school to notice the disc being nicked in the first place.)

WHICH MEANS! Izzy's list will also be a list of suspects! (Because everyone else will have gone home by the time The Avenger struck.)

BUT! If The Purple Avenger had to remove the disc from Jeremy's bag . . . Why not just steal it? Why risk being spotted putting it back? Why all The Purple Avenger bit? Unless the note is a fake clue, to throw suspicion AWAY from Jeremy. Which implies that . . . Jeremy . . . did it . . . himself . . .

It looks more and more like Jeremy DID do it himself. For whatever reason. He IS our class's only reader of *The Purple Avenger* comics. Maybe he didn't want to give in his essay because he thought it wasn't very good? No, not at all likely. Besides, nobody HAS to enter the competition, it's purely by choice.

Fact: I am very confused.

CHAPTER FOUR

ON THE WAY INTO school the next morning, I passed the caretaker's ladder. Once again, it was propped up beside the leaky roof over the toilets. The caretaker was slapping on the waterproof DIY sealing thingummy whatsit with a huge, sticky-looking brush. And the sticky-looking bit was purple.

'Morning, Mr Gumm!' I called.

He gave me a nod.

'Er, Mr Gumm,' I continued, 'you haven't, by any chance, possibly, maybe, had some of that waterproof DIY sealing thingummy whatsit nicked, have you?'

His head suddenly popped into sight over the edge of the roof. 'Yes!' he said. 'I had the end of a pot of it go missing the other day. How did . . .? Hang on, was it you? It was you, wasn't it?!'

'No, I'm just a brilliant detective!'

'Oh yeah? Who's your form teacher? What's your name? You thieving little monster! Oi, come back here!'

I legged it. Quick.

At least I'd all-but-confirmed what The Purple Avenger had used to purple that disc. However, as soon as I got to class, the happiness I felt at my own cleverness fizzled away like air escaping from a balloon.

The bell was about to go. Mrs Penzler was about to arrive. The entire class stood frozen to the spot, mouths gaping, staring at the large sheet of paper that Izzy had pulled from her desk.

Yesterday, this piece of paper had been covered in a complicated hand-drawn diagram. Today, it was covered in purple goo. And slapped into the centre of the now-dry goo was a note, printed on top of a cut-out section of comic book:

THE PURPLE AVENGER
STRIKES AGAIN!
TEE HEE!

At that moment, the entire class gave the second in their trilogy of loud gasps! Izzy Moustique was furious. 'That took me DAYS!' she wailed.

'Oh dear,' smarmed Harry Lovecraft. 'Looks like Moustique's out of the running in the competition too.'

I glanced at Jeremy Sweetly. He was trying so hard to look

innocent that he might just as well have had *IT WAS ME! GUILTY!* stamped across his face. He was going redder in the cheeks than a toddler who's just done something nasty in his pants.

'Dear me,' oozed Harry Lovecraft. 'Looks like this Purple Avenger is getting the better of our class detective.'

Everyone looked in my direction. 'I'm following up a number of important leads,' I said grandly. I don't think they believed me. I didn't even believe me.

Izzy came over, holding out the ruined paper. 'Saxby, you've got to catch this person!'

'Are you really out of the competition?' I said.

'I can re-do this sheet,' said Izzy, 'but it's going to take ages. I might not finish in time. Essays have got to be handed in at the end of this week, remember.'

'Did you get any info out of the note that was stuck on Jeremy's disc?'

'Not much. I can't tell exactly what comic book the paper came from, not without weeks of searching. The font that the message was printed with – and this second message too, by the look of it – is a standard one that's on all the school's computers. And on half the computers in the world, probably. Actually, the word "font" is incorrect. You should use the word "typeface", because in lettering a "font" is —'

'Yes, yes,' I said. 'OK, so the message is a dead end. Did

you manage to get a list of everyone that was here after school hours the night of the first Purple Avenger attack?'

'Yup, no problem.'

'I'll need a list of everyone who was here last night too.'

'Of course! You can cross-reference them. If someone was on both lists . . .'

'They had the opportunity to commit both crimes!' I said. 'That will narrow the list of suspects down even further.'

Izzy spent that morning's break time at the school office, getting hold of all the relevant information. I spent that morning's break time dodging the caretaker. He wanted his missing pot of waterproof DIY sealing thingummy whatsit, and he wouldn't take 'I didn't do it!' for an answer.

Once we were all back in class, Izzy gave me the lists. She'd thought ahead, and got hold of a list covering today (Wednesday) as well, just in case.

I checked through the lists while I sat gasping for breath. I'd run halfway around the school escaping that caretaker. 'I am *so* unfit!' I wheezed to myself.

As I looked at these lists, I was able to make an exact list of suspects: there were four people who could have committed both crimes.

Does your list match mine?

MONDAY LIST OF AFTER-SCHOOL ACTIVITIES
The following have permission to be on school premises.

DANCE CLUB Mrs Womsey Upper School Hall	COMPUTER CLUB Mr Nailshott ICT suite	SCHOOL BAND Mrs Penzler Lower School Hall
Susanne Foreman	Isobel Moustique	Scott Carey
Becky Wright	James McCrimmon	Anne Darrow
Jeremy Sweetly	Iain Chesterton	Michael Carpenter
Joanne Grant	Barry Sullivan	Laura Palmer
Sarah Smith	Alison Lethbridge	Matthew Ronay
Zoe Halibutt	Harry Lovecraft	Rob Blake
Vicki Waterfield	Li Chang	Jennifer Stannis
Liz Short	George Litefoot	Keith Avon
Sophie Tate	Henry Jago	Olag Travis
Imogen Watkins	Emma Buller	Kathy O'Rac

TUESDAY LIST OF AFTER-SCHOOL ACTIVITIES
The following have permission to be on school premises.

ART CLUB Mrs Vesey Art Room	SCHOOL NEWSLETTER Mrs Clements ICT suite	FOOTBALL CLUB Mr Hartright Lower School field
Paulo Pesca		William Kemp
Isobel Moustique	Jenny Maple	Jack Stapleton
Jeremy Sweetly	Bob Bell	Jonathan Small
Jasmine Winchester	Ella Eccles	John McFarlane
Anne Catherick	Sophie Tate	Charles Milverton
Percy Glyde	Netta Longdon	Ed Baldwin
Laura Fairlie	Harvey Bone	Harry Lovecraft
Vincent Gilmore	Vicki Pike	Henry Baker
Marian Halcombe	Joe Stangerson	Alex Holder
Liza Michelson	Lucy Ferrier	Susan Cushing
	Alice Turner	

The list was:

- Jeremy Sweetly
- That low-down rat Harry Lovecraft
- Izzy
- Sophie Tate

Izzy didn't seem a likely Avenger. She'd been the victim of Purple Avenger attack number two, plus if she was guilty she'd hardly have left her own name on those lists for me to discover.

Sophie Tate was someone I hadn't considered. She wasn't part of my usual circle of buddies, but as far as I knew she certainly wasn't the type to start covering people's CDs and carefully-made diagrams in purple goo. All I really knew about her was the fact that she always wore chunky shoes with great thick soles on them. And that didn't seem like a very helpful fact at all!

That low-down rat Harry Lovecraft was still top of the list, as far as I was concerned. I had no proof whatsoever, and nothing except my own suspicions to link him to The Purple Avenger. But these crimes were sneaky and spiteful, and anything sneaky and spiteful was Harry Lovecraft's speciality.

I checked through the after-school list for Wednesday. There was Jeremy Sweetly again on the list for Handicraft Club. There, also, was Harry Lovecraft, down for Chess

Club, *and* Sophie Tate, who was part of the school netball team. But no Izzy. (Izzy would have been down for Chess Club too, but they'd asked her to leave a couple of terms ago – nobody could beat her! She was still fuming over it.)

I was on the list too. Wednesdays were Book Club with Miss Bennett. That Wednesday was one I'd been looking forward to because we were going to do detective stories, and I had plenty to say on the subject (having read the huge library of crime fiction at home).

A brilliant idea popped into my head. At lunchtime, I did two things:

1. I apologised to Miss Bennett, and said I'd be late.
2. I made sure I was within earshot of Sophie Tate, Jeremy Sweetly and that low-down rat Harry Lovecraft, and talked loudly about how I was sure that The Purple Avenger would never dare purple MY essay, which by the way was tucked safely away in MY desk in THE CLASSROOM . . .

I also had a quick word with Muddy. I needed his help, as he was the school's resident inventor.

I'm sure you've spotted what my brilliant idea was?

Knowing that three of the four suspects on my list were going to be in school after hours, I was hoping to catch The Purple Avenger red-handed (well, purple-handed). My own essay was going to be used as bait!

The split second the bell went for the end of school, Muddy and I dashed for the gates and headed for his house.

A Page From My Notebook

Fact: The Purple Avenger is now out to knock more people than just Jeremy Sweetly out of the competition!

I suppose I could just wait until The Purple Avenger knocks everyone out of the competition except him/herself. *Then* I'd know who it was . . . But I wouldn't be much of a detective then, would I?

CHAPTER
FIVE

'HOW ABOUT THE WHITEHOUSE Long-Distance Grab Mechanism Mark Two?' said Muddy, wide-eyed with enthusiasm. 'I developed it from an old bike chain and a garden rake.'

Muddy Whitehouse was a master at anything mechanical, but getting him to hurry up was like trying to shift a giant boulder with a teaspoon.

'Muddy, no,' I gasped, 'thank you, no. I don't need any of that. I just need that camera you said you've got.'

It was ten minutes past the end of school. We'd dashed over to Muddy's place like a couple of rockets being chased by bigger rockets, and now we were in the garage attached to the side of his house (which is where he had his workshop). Or rather, as he liked to put it, his development laboratory.

The place was a tip. Covered in grime, littered with odds and ends, and full of half-finished ideas. Rather like Muddy himself, come to think of it.

'Quick, quick!' I wheezed, still out of breath from the run. 'I am sooo unfit! I haven't got long! Book Club is only an hour long, and I've got to get back and put this camera of yours in position yet!'

'Ah!' cried Muddy, holding up a finger, as if a light bulb had suddenly pinged into action above his head. 'How about the Whitehouse Laser Cutter 2000?'

He dug through an old cardboard box and pulled out a device that was half fighter aircraft plastic model kit, half battery pack. 'I adapted it from my mum's CD player. Of course, it doesn't actually cut things, as such. But there's a really cool little red light. Makes you look like a spy!'

'I'm not a spy,' I said quietly, 'I'm a detective. What on earth would I want a laser cutter for?'

'You could be a spy,' he said hopefully. 'I've got tons of great spy gear.'

'I don't want spy gear, I want a camera.'

'Cameras can be spy gear too.'

'Muuuuuudddddyyy!' I cried through gritted teeth. 'Camera! Please! Now!'

'OK,' muttered Muddy. 'Keep your hair on.' He opened a small cupboard that had once been part of a kitchen, and took out a camcorder. It was small and light, and so ideal for my purposes. It also had *Whitehouse VideoTron B* marked in serious-looking lettering on the side.

'The hard drive will store loads,' said Muddy, 'but the battery will need a recharge after an hour or so.'

'That's fine,' I said. 'An hour is plenty.'

'Of course, I rebuilt this thing from scratch. It dropped into a trifle last Christmas, but I managed to get every last bit of custard out of it.'

'This is brilliant! Thanks!' I shouted, already thirty metres away and heading back to school.

When I arrived back at our classroom, I quickly checked to see if my essay was safe. Luckily, it was still untouched. The Purple Avenger hadn't struck yet!

Nobody was about. Which was lucky, since they might have thought I was The Purple Avenger!

I placed the camcorder on the bottom shelf of the racking in the corridor outside the classroom (where lunchboxes and sports gear got dumped during the day). Here, it would be hidden from sight (unless The Purple Avenger was only about sixty centimetres high), and would have a perfect view of the classroom, and anyone entering or leaving it.

I set the recorder going. A tiny red light started blinking beside the lens. I gave it a quick wave and a grin, and hurried off to Book Club. I was still in time to amaze Miss Bennett and the rest of the club with the depth of my knowledge on detective fiction. Ta-daaa! The following morning, I could barely contain my giggles on the way to school. With a bit of luck, I'd be able to conclude the case in a matter of minutes.

I scooped up the camera while nobody was looking. Its battery had run down, and the light had stopped blinking. Nervously, I looked inside my desk. Had The Purple Avenger taken the bait? Was my essay now covered in waterproof DIY sealing thingummy whatsit?

W-w-was it . . .?

YES!

I peeled the ruined remains of my essay off the inside of my desk lid and held them up. Set into the middle of the goo was another of those notes:

THE PURPLE AVENGER
WILL ALWAYS WIN!
HO! HO!

Everyone spun around and stared. At that moment, the entire class gave the third and last in their trilogy of loud gasps. After they'd finished gasping, they started talking in low whispers about keeping their work under armed guard from now on.

'Hang on a minute,' I muttered to myself. 'I've just

spotted a flaw in my plan. Why didn't I put a dummy essay in my desk . . .?'

Making a muffled whining noise, I dropped the rubbery remains into the waste-paper basket. Izzy gave me a look which was one third sympathy, one third horror and one third why-didn't-you-put-a-dummy-essay-in-your-desk-you-silly-twit. Muddy gave me a big grin and a thumbs-up sign, and pointed at the camera.

That low-down rat Harry Lovecraft appeared at my shoulder, as if from nowhere. He was smiling like a python in a box of mice.

'Tut tut,' he slimed. 'This Purple Avenger has really got one over on you, hasn't he, Smart? Tut tut.'

I tried to think of a witty reply. But I couldn't, I was too busy seething with rage.

Muddy rooted around through the sweet wrappers in his pocket and produced a spare camcorder battery. 'Thought you could use this,' he said.

'Perfect!' I cried. 'Harry Lovecraft will be smirking on the other side of his shiny face when he realises I've caught him on camera!'

Quickly, I slotted the fresh battery into place and rewound the tape. While the rest of the class had moved on to talking in low whispers about keeping their essays in a bank vault until the end of the week, Iz and Muddy squashed up beside me to view the evidence.

'Right,' I said, pressing the Play button. 'This is the moment when I prove what a low-down rat Harry Lovecraft really is.'

On the camera's tiny flip-out screen, the video flicked into life. There was me, giving a grin and a wave at the camera . . . Aaaand I walk away . . . Aaaand we can clearly see the classroom door . . . Aaaand there's a long pause when nothing happens . . . Aaaand the picture goes tzzzttt.

'WHAT?' I cried.

Suddenly, the screen was filled with a crackly fuzz. All you could see was a thin strip of floor at the bottom of the picture.

'WHAT?' I cried.

'Awww,' said Muddy. 'It's always doing that. I think the custard must have damaged it more than I thought.'

'WHAT?' I cried again.

'Camcorders are very complicated,' said Muddy to Iz. 'He's lucky it works at all. I offered him the Whitehouse Laser Cutter 2000, but oooooh noooo, he didn't want that.'

They carried on yattering, while I peered at the little screen, trying to pick out whatever details I could.

Suddenly, my heart gave a twitch. There was a shadow appearing on the screen! Someone was sneaking into the classroom. I pressed Pause.

Almost all the image was a blur, but in the thin clear strip at the bottom I could see a pair of ordinary brown shoes, tiptoeing.

And at that moment, I knew who it was. I didn't need to see their face on the screen. By a process of elimination, I could work out which of the people on my suspect list was the guilty one.

My heart stopped twitching. It sank instead.

Have you worked it out?

It wasn't Izzy: she hadn't been in school after hours yesterday. It wasn't Sophie Tate: she wore shoes with thick soles. It wasn't Harry Lovecraft: his shoes were black and shiny. It could only have been Jeremy Sweetly.

The shoes on the video were rather stained and scuffed. Like a great slobbery dog might have chewed them here and there.

For the first time that morning, I looked over at Jeremy Sweetly. Or rather, I looked at his feet. Those shoes were unmistakable. I caught Jeremy's eyes. He could see what I was thinking, and I could see what he was thinking! He knew the game was up!

CHAPTER SIX

I HAD BEEN TOTALLY WRONG.

I simply *could not* believe it.

It really WAS him after all?

There *had* to be more to this than I was seeing.

At break time, I took Jeremy to one side. He knew I knew. And I knew he knew I knew.

'Jeremy, why?' I said.

He looked as if he was about to cry. Which, to be brutally honest, wasn't all that unusual for him. He'd looked as if he was about to cry when the class experiment in growing cress seeds had gone wrong.

'Why?' I said again. 'You're so sensible. And sensitive. And . . . some other things beginning with "s". Why?'

He made a dramatic shrug. 'Why not? I, umm, er, umm,

I was fed up of being sensible and sensitive. I thought I'd do something mean and nasty for a change.'

'To your own work?'

'Yes. *That's* how mean and nasty I can get! Even my own work isn't safe! Yeah! Mmm. Mean and nasty, that's me,' he said. He was completely unconvincing.

Then he said, 'Are you going to tell Mrs Penzler?'

'If I thought for one minute that you'd done it just to be mean and nasty, then yes, I would. But you didn't, did you? Who put you up to it, and why? Was it Harry Lovecraft?'

'No!' said Jeremy, rather too quickly.

I let the subject drop. Jeremy scampered away like a startled rabbit, clutching the latest issue of *The Purple Avenger* to his chest. He was scared, and it had nothing to do with being found out.

More than ever, I was sure Harry Lovecraft was at the bottom of this. But it wasn't simply a question of brute force. For one thing, Harry Lovecraft might have been sneaky, and sly, and underhand, but he wasn't the sort of bully who went in for rough, head-down-the-toilet stuff. He was much too fussy about his shiny hair and his spotless school uniform for that. He'd never dirty his hands by pushing little kids over on the sports field.

And for another thing, Jeremy Sweetly was no fool. If someone had started pushing him around, he'd have said so. He knew that bullies were always cowards, just as the rest of us did. There was something else going on. Something was keeping his mouth shut. Someone had some kind of hold over Jeremy Sweetly.

But what? Harry Lovecraft never had anything to do with Jeremy. The pair of them certainly weren't friends, they had no friends in common, and as far as I knew they'd hardly so much as exchanged hellos. (In fact, thinking about it, the most that Jeremy and Harry Lovecraft had ever interacted was early last term, when Jeremy caught him stealing someone's PE kit. Nothing unusual there. Izzy and I had reported him only a few weeks later, when he tried getting money off some younger kids by calling it 'School Dinner Tax'.)

Normally, people like Harry Lovecraft and people like Jeremy Sweetly just didn't bother with each other. The two of them didn't even live in the same part of town. What possible connection could there be?

I needed Izzy's help again. I needed information. There had to be some kind of link I was missing.

'What kind of link?' asked Izzy, puzzled.

'Some kind,' I said, looking all narrow-eyed and mysterious.

'And what if you're wrong?' said Izzy, doing a silly, goggle-eyed impression of my mysterious look.

'I'm never wrong,' I said.

But, I had to admit to myself, I could have been on a track that was more wrong than a London Underground train on the Trans-Siberian line!

However, during the course of that day I had two useful pieces of luck. Two pieces of luck which, it turned out, would solve the entire riddle.

CHAPTER
SEVEN

PIECE OF LUCK NUMBER ONE: a remark made by Harry Lovecraft as we were all coming back into the classroom after lunch time. Jeremy Sweetly had stepped through a puddle outside with those battered brown shoes of his. Harry Lovecraft, noticing Jeremy giving his foot a shake to help it dry out, smarmed past his desk saying, 'Hmmm, Sweetly's in need of new shoes again. Why don't you get Humphrey under control, Sweetly? Stop him chewing up the family footwear all the time. Hmmm?'

The deduction to be made from this remark didn't hit me at first. But then, as we all sat down and shuffled with our science folders ready for the lesson, it smacked me between the eyes like a cartoon anvil dropped off a cliff . . .

Even if Harry Lovecraft knew that Jeremy HAD a dog (and why would he even know that?), how would he know this dog's name, and that he kept 'chewing up the family footwear all the time'? Those were strangely precise snippets of information for Harry to have. You don't generally get to know a dog's bad habits unless you also happen to know the owner, do you? Or unless you've at least visited the owner.

Good grief, I thought to myself, Harry Lovecraft has *been to Jeremy's house*! (That low-down rat's visited my street, and I never realised! Eurgh!)

At first, this deepened the mystery even more. What in the name of Sherlock Holmes would Harry Lovecraft be doing at Jeremy Sweetly's house? But then came piece of luck number two.

Shortly after school Izzy emailed me. *Here's a piece of luck*, she wrote. *I had a quick read-through of Jeremy's winning essay from last year –* The Life Story of My Dad, *remember? It turned up some interesting background info. But that wasn't the piece of luck. The luck was that I did a search on the internet and came across something very similar which, I think you'll find, establishes a clear link between Harry and Jeremy.*

The 'something very similar' was a web page headed *Our Sales Team*, devoted to half a dozen shiny-looking people who all sold spare parts for cars for a living.

Can you spot the connection?

Rachel Verinder
Matthew Bruff
Donald Lovecraft
Franklin Blake
Rosanna Spearman
Andrew Sweetly

'That's *it*!' I cried. 'That's *it*!'

I didn't even need to retreat to my Thinking Chair for this one. I had all the answers.

The next day was essay-handing-in day. Everyone had their work ready and waiting at nine a.m. (Well, everyone except the victims of The Purple Avenger.)

Mrs Penzler marched in. 'I hope everyone's remembered their essay,' she announced, scanning the class with her pebble glasses. '"I left it on the bus" and "My baby sister ate it" are not acceptable excuses. Yes? Saxby?'

I'd raised my hand. 'Could I have a word with the whole class, before we go any further?'

'Is this an excuse for not handing in your essay, Saxby?' sighed Mrs Penzler.

'Umm . . . well, sort of . . . in a way,' I said.

'Then, sorry, no,' said Mrs Penzler.

'But what if I could reveal the real identity of The Purple Avenger?' I said. 'I can show that there's been cheating.'

The class all leaned forward, eyes wide. 'Well, all right then,' said Mrs Penzler. 'But you'd better be right.'

I stood at the front, underneath the interactive board. Everyone stared at me. Harry Lovecraft looked smug and confident. Jeremy Sweetly looked terrified.

I tried to give Jeremy a look which said, 'Don't worry, I won't get you into trouble.' But I really wasn't sure how to do that, so I think I ended up giving him a look which said, 'Just you wait and see.' Which I don't think reassured him very much.

'The identity of The Purple Avenger is . . .'

I paused for dramatic effect. The whole class leaned forward even more, eyes even wider. I couldn't pause for long, or eyes would start falling out.

'. . . going to have to remain a secret.'

The whole class groaned. Harry Lovecraft looked more smug and confident than ever. Jeremy Sweetly looked relieved.

'But!' I cried, one finger in the air. Everyone shut up. 'The person responsible for The Purple Avenger attacks was *forced* to do what he did. Er, or she did. Umm, look, I'll call this person Person X, OK?

'Right. Person X purpled the work of Jeremy Sweetly, Isobel Moustique and me. But Person X did *not* do these things voluntarily. Person X was being threatened. You see, Person X has a dog. A big, slobbery hound, which Person X loves beyond all reason. However, this dog is always wandering around the neighbourhood. No matter what Person X does to keep him at home, the dog keeps escaping and getting himself into trouble. Now here's where Harry Lovecraft enters the scene . . .'

Everyone turned and stared at Harry Lovecraft. Mrs

Penzler said, 'Saxby, you'd better be careful!' Harry Lovecraft didn't so much as twitch. He just gazed at me.

'Harry Lovecraft would normally have nothing whatsoever to do with Person X. But it just so happens that there is a connection. Not so much a connection between them, but a connection between their *parents*.

'It's a matter of public record – umm, I can't quite say *how* in Person X's case, 'cos that'll give away who Person X is – anyway, it's a matter of public record that Person X's dad, and Harry Lovecraft's dad work at the same company, a company which makes and sells spare parts for cars.

'These dads both work in the Sales Team. One day they got together outside work. Harry Lovecraft's family went over to Person X's house. Harry Lovecraft and Person X, two people who would never, ever normally go anywhere near each other, were suddenly in the same social circle.

'So Harry Lovecraft gets to meet this slobbery great dog. And he realises that this dog is Person X's weakness. If he wanted to get Person X to do something, he wouldn't have to thump him or anything. Oh, no. All he'd have to do is drop nasty little hints about the dog getting out all the time, and about the dog maybe getting *lost*, maybe getting lost *for ever*. You see what I'm getting at?

'So along comes the essay competition. Harry Lovecraft

spots an opportunity. Person X is the favourite to win, and
. . . Oh dear.'

I'd blown it. Everyone stared at Jeremy Sweetly. Jeremy
Sweetly went redder than a sunburnt tomato.

'Oh, bum,' I said. 'Yeah, OK, it's Jeremy Sweetly. Let's
move on. Sorry, Jeremy. Harry Lovecraft sees he can
remove Jeremy from the competition, by simply making
threats about poor Jeremy's beloved dog.

'Now, this is where I went wrong. I assumed, as we all
did, that The Purple Avenger was out to nobble the front-
runners in the essay competition. But that wasn't it at all. The
competition had nothing to do with it. The competition was
just a convenient opportunity. It was a matter of revenge.

'Last term, you'll recall, Jeremy found Harry Lovecraft
stealing someone else's PE kit. Naturally, Harry got into big
trouble for it. The essay competition was Harry's chance to
get even, as he saw it. Jeremy was the favourite to win.
What better revenge, thinks Harry to himself, than to spoil
Jeremy's chance at winning.

'But Harry Lovecraft, being Harry Lovecraft, can't just
make Jeremy drop out of the competition, and leave it at
that. Oh no. He wants his revenge to be a little more
painful, a little more public. He's been to Jeremy's house,
and he's seen that Jeremy reads *The Purple Avenger* comics.
So Harry nicks some sealant stuff from the school caretaker,

and he makes poor Jeremy destroy his own work, do it in the name of his favourite superhero, and show the world the results.

'You see, that was Harry's first mistake. The first of two. If he'd quietly made Jeremy miss out on the essay competition, we might never have known what was going on. Without the ruined disc, and the message, even I might not have suspected foul play. Harry might have continued making Jeremy's life miserable for ages. But no. Harry had to be Harry. He had to be cruel. In a way, he set up his own downfall.

'But at first, he got away with it. Nothing pointed to Harry Lovecraft as being the guilty party. If anyone was going to get into trouble this time, it was Jeremy. So Harry gets greedy. Who else do I want revenge on, he thinks? Who reported him for his nasty little "School Dinner Tax" scheme? Time for The Purple Avenger to strike Isobel's work, and mine. And if Jeremy gets found out, so what? If Jeremy starts pointing the finger at Harry, then all Harry has to do is make his threats all over again. Harry thinks he's in the clear.'

Slowly, everyone turned to look at Harry Lovecraft. Now, Harry Lovecraft was looking extremely uncomfortable.

'So,' said Mrs Penzler quietly, 'what was Harry's second mistake?'

'Oh, that's easy,' I said, even more quietly. 'He didn't reckon on Saxby Smart.'

For a moment or two there was total silence. Then Mrs Penzler adjusted her glasses and barked, 'Harry Lovecraft, Jeremy Sweetly, is this true?'

Harry had nowhere to hide. Now that his threats were in the open, Jeremy had no reason to cover up for him.

'Yes,' said Jeremy, bravely.

'Yes,' croaked Harry Lovecraft, through gritted teeth.

There was uproar in the classroom. Once it had all died down, two things happened. First, Harry Lovecraft was sent to the head's office. Second, Mrs Penzler talked to the head about postponing the handing-in of essays until The Purple Avenger's victims could have a chance to re-do their work.

'Thanks, Saxby,' said Jeremy at lunch time.

He gave me a soppy smile, and I think I spotted a tear in his eye so I quickly said, 'All in a day's work,' and hurried off to talk to Muddy.

For the rest of the day, I felt pretty good about things. I'd solved a puzzling mystery, and everyone thought I was pretty cool. When I got home, I headed straight for my shed. I wanted to jot down some notes on the case while they were fresh in my mind.

Humphrey was flopped out in his favourite spot, right

in front of the shed door. I spoke sharply. I spoke nicely. I whistled. I growled. I tried to tempt the drooling mutt away with a choccie biccie. Nothing.

'Jeremmmmyyyyyy!' I yelled across the road.

Case closed.

CASE FILE THREE:

THE CLASP
OF DOOM

CHAPTER
ONE

THERE ARE SOME PEOPLE you meet who simply make you smile. The sort of people who light up a room just by walking into it. The sort of people who make everyone around them feel happy.

Mrs Eileen Pither was *not* one of them.

Legend had it that she'd spent thirty-five years working for the local council, turning orphans out into the street and counting stacks of coins in deep, dark dungeons. But all that was years ago. At the time of the case of *The Clasp of Doom* she spent all her time organising her fellow old ladies, and writing to the papers about the terrible state of the roads, and how young people today had no manners.

Everyone in town knew Mrs Eileen Pither. And Mrs Eileen Pither knew everyone.

It was a wet, miserably grey day in the Easter holidays. A girl from the Year below me at school, Heather Gardens, called on me in my garden shed. She knocked, and the *Saxby Smart – Private Detective: KEEP OUT* sign dropped off the door, as usual. I made a mental note to get that thing nailed up properly once and for all, and sat Heather down on my desk. I flopped into my Thinking Chair and took up a steeple-fingered pose, in order to look intelligent and detectivey.

'How can I help you?' I said. 'Apart from doing your homework on plants, that is. But I'll leave that to you.'

She blinked at me. 'How on earth did you know I've been doing homework on plants?' she said.

'There are spots of green paint on your fingers, and the fresh sticking plaster on your left thumb shows you've got a slight cut there. Painting and cutting suggests making something. You're in the Year below me at school, which means you're very likely to have been given the same homework these holidays that I was, this time last year. Which involved making a model plant. Bit of a guess, but I see I was right. Now, how can I help?'

Heather was a dark-haired girl with a slight build and a face dotted with freckles. At the time, her face was also dotted with worry.

'I'm related to Mrs Eileen Pither,' she said with a shudder.

Thunder rumbled overhead.

'I'm so sorry,' I said. 'I had no idea.'

She shook her head, her eyes screwed up. 'It's OK, really. I just don't talk about it, that's all. She's my mum's aunt.'

'And she's caused some sort of problem, I presume? Is that why you're here?'

'Yes,' she said. 'You've heard what a sour-tempered person she is?'

'Who hasn't?' I muttered.

'She's accused me of stealing her jewellery. She's threatening to go to the police.'

The thunder rumbled all over again.

CHAPTER
TWO

'GIVE ME THE WHOLE STORY, start to finish,' I said. I leaned forward in my Thinking Chair. Rain spattered down the shed window.

'Mrs Pither comes to our house every now and again. She keeps getting my mum to join organising committees for various charities. Anyway, Mrs Pither turned up to organise Mum last Saturday, and as she was leaving, she suddenly turned around, in the doorway, and pointed at me. "Where is my antique clasp?" she demanded. I hadn't the faintest idea. She started getting angry, and said I must have stolen it.'

'What does this clasp look like?' I asked.

'It's a hideous thing,' said Heather, wrinkling her nose. 'It's in the form of two hands, sort of curled around each other. They're made of silver, with little diamonds set into the fingers. There's a big, sharp pin-type clip at the back. She uses it to hold the sides of her coat together, a ratty old thing.'

'Yes, I've heard she is,' I mumbled.

'No, the coat is a ratty old thing! It's green, and it stinks of mothballs. She's never without it. I think she's too mean to put new buttons on it, which is why she uses that clasp.'

'She had it when she arrived?' I said.

'Oh, yes,' said Heather. 'I saw it. Right there, clipped on at chest level. She thought I was admiring it! I kept myself busy in my room while she and Mum were talking, and I happened to come downstairs just as she was leaving.'

'I presume the coat, with the clasp, was hanging up somewhere while she was with your mum?'

'Yes,' said Heather. 'In the hall. She put the coat back on, stepped out of the front door, and then must have noticed the clasp was missing.'

'And how long was the coat hanging in the hall?'

'About an hour.'

'And *could* anyone have stolen it?'

'Well, yes, I suppose someone *could* have taken it during that time. But apart from Mrs Pither and Mum, there were only me and my elder brother in the house.'

'Nobody could have sneaked in?'

'Mum would have seen anybody coming to the front of the house from where she was sitting. And I would have seen anybody at the back because my room overlooks the garden.'

'And I assume the clasp has been searched for?' I said.

'*Everywhere!*' cried Heather. 'My mum and I scoured the house. There's no sign of it.'

'You're sure she didn't lose it somewhere outside the house?'

'No. She definitely had it on when she arrived. It definitely wasn't there when she left. We even searched in her nephew's car! She makes him drive her wherever she wants to go, because she can't drive herself. She burdens him with guilt by playing the I'm-a-poor-feeble-old-lady card. He's softer than melted butter.'

'He didn't come into the house?'

'No, he was off doing her shopping for her the whole time. He'd just arrived to pick her up.'

I sat back in my Thinking Chair. 'Very odd,' I muttered. 'I wonder why Mrs Pither would assume it had been stolen? And stolen by you?'

Heather shrugged. 'Because she's mean?'

'Hmm, yes, could be,' I agreed.

'I think it's because she thought I was admiring it when she arrived. She's never liked me,' said Heather. 'Mind you, she doesn't like anybody under the age of about a hundred and fifty. And now she's convinced I've taken this clasp of hers.'

'Is it valuable?' I asked.

'I don't know,' said Heather. 'It didn't *look* valuable. It looked ugly. I can't imagine anyone paying so much as a penny for the horrible thing.'

'And you say Mrs Pither is threatening to go to the police?' I asked. 'Surely she has no evidence?'

'I think she's more interested in making a public fuss than anything else. Causing maximum embarrassment. It'll all kick off first thing Monday morning, if the clasp isn't returned to her. She said to my mum, "I'll give that girl until then to come to her senses and confess".'

'And she'll really do it?'

'Without a shadow of a doubt,' said Heather sadly. 'She bursts kids' footballs if they land on her lawn, and she tried to sue her neighbours for having a barbecue. She's not going to think twice about getting me into trouble. She's already started gossiping to her committees about me! It's not fair! I'm really worried!'

'Never fear,' I said. 'Saxby Smart is on the case!'

A Page From My Notebook

Fact: The clasp definitely came INTO Heather's house.
Fact: It was gone before Mrs Pither LEFT the house.
Fact: It's been searched for INSIDE the house.

Possibility 1: It's vanished into thin air. Hmm, not very likely.
Possibility 2: Heather really did steal it. Hmm, also not very likely. Why would she involve me, if she was guilty?
Possibility 3: Mrs Pither could be attempting an insurance scam! She could be pretending it's been stolen, to get money out of an insurance company.
Possibility 4: The clasp got dropped through a hole in the floorboards.
Possibility 5: Heather's elder brother is involved; he's the only other person In the frame, but as yet I know nothing about him.

Plan
I need to find out more about Mrs Pither, about this clasp and about Heather's brother. I also need to examine the scene of the crime . . .

CHAPTER
THREE

I EMAILED MY SUPER-INTELLIGENT FRIEND, Izzy, gave a detailed description of the clasp along with a rough sketch done by Heather, and asked her to track down whatever useful information she could. I also made arrangements with Heather to visit her house the following day, to examine the scene of the crime.

The next day was the wettest and dreariest for ages; the sort of day when the clouds look like wet tissues, and the rain makes an endless roaring noise against the roof.

Heather lived in a very ordinary-looking house, in a very ordinary-looking street. Rain drummed on the lids of the recycling bins, put out all along the street for collection.

When I arrived, I thought that the look of misery on her mum's face might be either dismay at the theft of the clasp, or else dismay at the horrible weather. But I was wrong on both counts.

'Mrs Pither's on her way over,' said Heather with a shudder.

'Excellent!' I cried.

Heather's mum looked at me as if I was slightly mad. 'Why, Saxby?' she gasped.

'Because I'd like to ask her some questions,' I said. 'If I'm going to investigate a —'

'Here!' interrupted Heather's mum, thrusting a duster into my hands. 'Polish the stair rail. She'll run her finger along it. If there's any dust, she'll make a sarcastic comment.'

Heather whispered to me, 'Mrs Pither's got more committee stuff for Mum to do. My mum's too nice. If only she'd stop doing charity work around here then we'd only ever see that woman at major family events.'

I polished the stair rail. Heather swept the floors. Her mum tidied the living room and made sure there were the right number of cushions on the sofa for Mrs Pither to sit comfortably.

While I polished, I took a close look at the hallway. Beside the front door was a set of hooks, holding a couple of coats, a scarf and a woolly hat. Opposite the coat hooks was a small table, scattered with assorted keys, a couple of items of mail, and reminders scribbled on scraps of paper. There was a little jar containing loose change, and a small pile of money-off vouchers for the local shops. Above the table was a mirror in a broad wooden frame.

The floors were made of that tough, wooden-looking stuff (so no holes in floorboards for clasps to get dropped into). The floor showed, as you'd expect, a faint pattern of scuff marks around the busy areas (with, I noticed with a smile, neatly rectangular untouched patches where nobody had walked, one beneath the table and a larger one under the coat hooks). The stairs, where I was busy polishing, began near the hall table, and a short corridor led to the living room and kitchen. Along the corridor hung three abstract paintings (a bit ugly, I thought) marked *TG* in the bottom right corners.

All very ordinary-looking. And not a single clue to be had from any of it. Or was there? I could tell that something was missing! How did I know?

I pointed to the coat hooks. 'Something normally sits under those hooks, a box of some kind. There wouldn't be a big untouched patch of floor there otherwise. Not a neat, rectangular patch, anyway.'

'Just the recycling box,' said Heather. 'It's out on the kerb at the moment – it's collection day.'

'Ah!' I said. 'Yes. I saw it on my way in. And . . .?'

'Yeeees, it was searched,' said Heather. 'Mum searched it. Everywhere was searched.'

Through the ripple-glassed panels in the front door, I could see a car pull up outside. Heather's mum bustled out of the living room. 'Here we go,' she mumbled. She took a deep breath and swung the door open.

Mrs Pither was busy organising her nephew. He was to go and collect her new wardrobe from the furniture shop, then take it back to her house, then put it together, and then come back to collect her. The car pulled away quickly.

'Hello, Eileen,' said Heather's mum.

Mrs Pither was wearing the tatty old green coat that Heather had described to me, all threadbare and frayed at the edges. It flapped down to the level of her ankles, not because it was particularly long, but because she was particularly short. She clacked along in low-heeled shoes, her big feet duck-waddling at the end of stick-like legs. Her white hair appeared to have been gruesomely attacked with hairspray, and her face had the permanent look of having just drunk a glass of lemon juice.

'Morning,' she barked, as if the word was rude. She spoke to Heather's mum, ignoring Heather and me completely. 'Have you made enough people volunteer for next week yet?'

'Yes, four,' said Heather's mum.

'That's not enough,' argued Mrs Pither. 'Here, hang my coat up, would you? Of course, I've been freezing in it, because I can't do it up, not since my clasp was stolen. Have you taken the collection tins to the building society yet?'

'Yes, of course I have, Eileen, now about —'

'Glad to hear it. You can't be too careful, with thieves lurking around every corner. What's wrong with your heating? It's like ice in here.'

She waddled along the hall to the living room, running a finger along the stair rail and finding no dust. She made no comment. Heather's mum shut her eyes for a moment. 'It's for charity,' she muttered to herself. 'It's all for charity . . .'

She whispered to us to go and put the kettle on, then followed Mrs Pither. Heather and I scurried to the kitchen.

'Hmm,' I said, fetching the biscuits. 'I'm surprised I'm not investigating a murder.'

'Oh, she's in a good mood today,' said Heather. 'You should see her when she's being a misery.'

The front door bumped, and a few moments later Heather's older brother came rumbling along the hall and into the kitchen. It turned out that he was eighteen years old, that his name was Tim, and that he was a student at the nearby college.

'H'lo,' he said to me, with a nod, dumping a handful of library books on to the worktop. He clunked about the kitchen making a sandwich. He was obviously one of those people who can't do anything without making a noise and leaving a mess. Even his shoes, and the bottom half of his jeans, were covered with multi-coloured spots that had clearly been there for ages.

'Did you hear about Mrs Pither's clasp?' I asked him.

'Y'h,' he said. 'She's prob'ly left it under her cat or somethin'.'

As I picked up the tray of tea and biscuits, I took a quick look at Tim's library books. Only one was turned so that I could see the title: *Costume Jewellery: Current Price Lists and Valuations*.

That was odd. Jewellery? Why would he want to find out about the value of jewellery?

Unless he had the clasp, and wanted to discover what it was worth? Could *he* have stolen it?

113

He gathered up his stuff and set off upstairs, chewing his sandwich. He dropped breadcrumbs and little splats of jam as he went. As soon as he was out of earshot, I said to Heather, 'Was Tim in his room when the clasp was stolen?'

'Yes, that whole afternoon,' Heather replied.

Why? Why would Tim want to steal the clasp? Or, more to the point, need the money, since he was apparently trying to find out its value? An idea struck me. Suddenly, I realised why he might be in particular need of money.

'Tim spends a lot of money on stuff for his college course, doesn't he? Stuff that gets used up?' I said.

'Yes,' said Heather. 'He owes Mum a small fortune. How on earth did you know that? I've not even told you what he's studying.'

Heather didn't need to tell me anything about what subject Tim was studying at college. I'd worked that one out already. Have you?

'He's studying art,' I said. 'There are abstract paintings hanging in the hall signed *TG*. That *could* be someone other than Tim Gardens, but the multi-coloured dots all over his shoes and jeans are probably paint. What else would come in lots of colours? So he's an art student. And paint, canvas, brushes and so on don't come cheap.'

Heather smiled and shook her head. 'Jasmine Winchester said you were always one step ahead. Anyway, why do you need to know what he spends on art stuff?'

I didn't think it was a good idea to tell Heather about my suspicions. Not yet. After all, suspicions weren't proof.

'Oh, nothing, just interested,' I said. 'Come on, let's take this tea in!'

In the living room, Mrs Pither was organising Heather's mum like a Reception teacher organising a finger-painting session. Heather's mum kept scribbling notes in a thick jotter pad.

I set the tea tray down on the coffee table in front of them. Heather's mum gave me a big grin which said 'Thank you' and also 'Help me, someone, she's driving me mad.' Heather quickly put the biscuits on the tray and hurried out to escape Mrs Pither. Mrs Pither looked at the tray as if she'd ordered something expensive in a posh restaurant and been served poo and tap water. I made myself comfy. I wasn't going anywhere, I still had questions to ask.

'Is this tea freshly brewed?' snapped Mrs Pither. 'I'm a very delicate person. My innards can't take tea that's been allowed to stew in the pot.'

'It's as fresh as a daisy that's just this minute popped out of the lawn,' I said.

For the first time, Mrs Pither looked directly at me. I flinched. It was like being stared at by a cobra.

'Who are you?' she said.

'This is Saxby, a friend of Heather's,' said Heather's mum. 'He's come to help find this lost clasp of yours.'

'Ah! Has that girl come to her senses yet? Has she confessed?'

'Eileen,' said Heather's mum, pulling back her chin in a now-just-a-minute expression, 'I've told you, Heather does not have your clasp. We're all very sorry it's missing, but—'

'I'm a very forgiving person,' snapped Mrs Pither. 'If she returns the item to me, with her express apologies, then I'll only ask the police to caution her. But, as I have told you, if I don't get my clasp back by ten o'clock Monday morning, things will get a lot more serious!'

A bleeping sound was thankfully drowning her out a bit – a lorry was backing up, collecting everyone's recycling bin out in the street.

'Mrs Pither,' I said. 'Could I ask you a few questions about that clasp?'

'No you may not,' she barked. 'Who are you again?'

'Saxby.'

'What a ridiculous name,' she muttered.

I did my own bit of chin-pulling-in. 'I'm investigating the disappearance of your clasp.'

'Are you indeed?' she piped. 'This isn't a silly game, you know. Run along home with you!' She started rubbing her ankle. It certainly looked rather sore. 'It's been bitten raw by insects for days! Does this sofa have fleas?'

'What?' cried Heather's mum. 'Of course not!'

There was a distant bumping of plastic boxes from further down the street, as the recycling bins were emptied. Heather's mum gulped down her tea to stop herself from saying something that would make her as rude as her guest.

'If I could just ask about this clasp?' I enquired politely. 'Did you have a handbag with you the other day? One the clasp could have been put into by mistake?'

'A handbag?' cried Mrs Pither, her eyes stretching free of the wrinkles around them. 'No I did not! Do you take me for a fool, boy? My clasp was stolen by that girl!'

'I'm telling you, Eileen,' said Heather's mum, 'nobody in this house would steal anything!'

I said nothing.

'Well someone in this house did,' said Mrs Pither.

117

'Mrs Pither,' I said, 'did you go to the loo while you were here? Or out into the garden? I'm just trying to establish your movements.'

Her eyes were on the point of dropping out and plopping into her tea.

'Honestly, Saxby,' said Heather's mum, 'we've covered all that. Heather and I searched the entire house, wherever Mrs Pither had been or not.'

'You did it between you?'

'Yes, I looked on the stairs, the front drive, in the kitchen, and the hall. Heather did in here, the hall cupboard, the recycling box, the coats and shoes, out the back, in the —'

I leapt to my feet!

There had been a mix-up. Something *had* been missed!

'Oh *no!*' I yelled. I took a jump towards the window, realised I was wasting precious time, jumped towards the door instead and dashed out of the house. Heather, who was coming down the stairs, quickly followed me.

'What is it?' she called.

A rubbish collector was, at that moment, emptying the recycling box from the hall into one of the big green bins that filled the back of the lorry. My yell of 'Stoooooppp!' was drowned out by the revving of the lorry's engine. It rumbled away faster than I could run.

'But we searched the recycling box!' said Heather.

'Who searched it?' I cried.

'I told you before. Mum did.'

'Exactly! She just said *you* did. That box was right under where Mrs Pither's coat was hanging up.' I pointed madly at the rapidly departing lorry. 'The clasp must be *on that truck!*'

CHAPTER FOUR

I HAD TO THINK QUICKLY! There was no way I could go back inside the house and say, 'Oops, sorry, Mrs P, your antique jewellery is on its way to be recycled.'

Luckily, I'd spotted which of the green bins the recycling box had been emptied into. The only hope was to intercept that bin *before* it got emptied out again.

I kind of skipped about for a second or two, not knowing what to do, looking like a complete twit and making little 'argh' noises. But then I had an idea.

'Muddy!' I cried at last. 'Muddy lives in the next street!'

Leaving Heather looking bemused, I dashed to Muddy's house. He was in his garage (otherwise known as his Development Laboratory), taking a broken DVD player apart.

'Muddy!' I gasped, almost tumbling over as I skidded to a halt.

'Hi Saxby,' he said, not looking up from his work. 'Sorry, delicate operation, whatever you do, don't jog my elbow.'

'I need that bike you adapted, quick!' I wheezed. I added to myself: 'And I've got to get more exercise.'

'The Whitehouse Speedy 4000?' said Muddy, keeping his eyes firmly on what he was doing. 'Over in the corner. Why do you need it?'

'I'm on a case,' I cried, grabbing the bike and the helmet that dangled from its handlebars. 'I have to follow a lorry.'

Muddy suddenly looked up with a big grin on his face. The delicate piece of electronics he'd been examining toppled over on to the floor. 'Ooh,' he said. 'You might want the Whitehouse Super-View Zoom-Glasses, too? They're made from binoculars and a pair of my dad's specs.'

'No thanks.'

'Or some Whitehouse Ultra-Headlamps?'

'It's broad daylight! How long do you think I'm going to be chasing this lorry? Sorry, GOT to go! I'll bring the bike back later!'

I sped away at top speed, before he could start going on about spy gear. The Whitehouse Speedy 4000 had specially-adapted gears: once you'd got it going (and that took an effort, because of the bigger cog-wheel-thingummy beside the pedals), it flew along on its extra-chunky tyres like lightning. Plus it had rather cool flame graphics painted on it!

The recycling lorry was way out of sight. For a big truck, it was a fast mover; I'd seen it plenty of times in the past, rumbling along from street to street, hardly ever stopping, with workmen dashing about collecting bins all around it. It was like worker ants feeding a giant, lumbering queen with old newspapers and tin cans.

The trouble was, I didn't know what route it took. The roads in this area were a winding criss-cross of streets. It would be very easy to lose track of it completely. As I cycled along, I strained to hear the echo of its engine. But the noise from the nearby main road made it impossible to pick out a specific vehicle.

I looked around me for clues. Of course! There was one very simple method of working out where the lorry had (or hadn't) been . . .

I could track it by looking at which streets' bins had been emptied, and which hadn't. Using this method, I caught up with the lorry after about a kilometre or so. Even then, I had to cycle like mad to keep up.

It occurred to me that I could cut across town, go straight to the local recycling plant, and meet the lorry there. However, there was a serious flaw in that plan: I'd need to distinguish this lorry from all the others there. Even if I took a note of its number plate, I could easily miss it.

No, I'd have to follow it. There was no alternative. As I pedalled for all I was worth, two thoughts struck me:

1. I was glad that my suspicions about Tim had been wrong. It would have been very unpleasant to have had to reveal to Heather and her mum that there was a thief in their house after all.

2. I was going to have to search through a load of recycling to find this bloomin' clasp! The things we detectives have to do!

I managed to keep pace with the lorry – just – until it headed for the recycling plant. I was finally able to get ahead of it, and was waiting when it rumbled to a halt outside the gates of the plant, its brakes hissing.

'Oi!' called the driver. 'You're not allowed past those gates, lad!'

I launched into my prepared speech. I told the workmen

that I'd accidentally thrown away a treasured newspaper clipping about how I'd rescued a dog called Humphrey from drowning. (I didn't want to tell them the truth, just in case one of them got greedy, sent me packing, and started looking for a valuable item of jewellery for themselves.) 'Please, mister, please please please, oh please, I know where it is, it's in that bin there, mister, please.'

And so on, and so on. The workmen looked at each other as if to say 'This boy is a complete idiot'.

'Gooo on, then,' said the driver. 'Empty the bin over on the grass there. And put every last bit back afterwards. Right?'

'Right! No problem! Thank you!' I said, beaming.

'Leave the bin by the gate when you've finished. And don't be such a complete idiot in future. I'm only letting you do this because of you being brave and saving that poor dog.'

'Understood.'

Once the gates had been opened and the lorry had thundered through, I emptied out the contents of the green bin.

The clasp was here somewhere, underneath all that old newspaper, tattered junk mail, torn-out pages and shredded paper. I wished I'd brought some gardening gloves from my shed.

I set to work. I carefully turned over each and every piece of junk, and then set it aside, making absolutely sure that nothing was missed, and that the clasp couldn't possibly stay undiscovered. After about half an hour, my hard work and effort were rewarded . . . with precisely nothing.

The clasp wasn't there. It had never been in that recycling box in the first place. I had been totally wrong

A Page From My Notebook

Fact: The clasp wasn't lost in the recycling box. It also cannot be found anywhere else in the house.

Conclusion: It MUST have been stolen after all.

Fact: Tim is the only one on my suspect list.

Awkward questions: How do I tell Heather?

How do I get proof?

How do I get the clasp back?

What if Tim's already sold it?

What will Mrs Pither do when she finds out?

CHAPTER
FIVE

ONCE I'D FINISHED GRUMBLING, griping and putting everything
back into the big green bin, I did three things:

1. I cycled back to Muddy's, returned the bike, and
washed all the newsprint stains off my hands.

2. I went back to Heather's, told her that I'd been wrong
about the recycling box, and said my investigations would
continue.

3. I went to Izzy's, to see if she had any info for me.

'Not very much, I'm afraid,' she said. 'That clasp is . . .
Are you listening?'

I was distracted for a moment. Since my last visit, Izzy
had hung one of those glittery mirrorball-things from her
ceiling. The twinkling reflections made her room look
even more colourful and girly than usual.

'Sorry,' I said. 'Yes, I'm listening.'

'That clasp could well be pretty valuable,' said Izzy. She consulted a set of print-outs and adjusted her glasses on her nose. 'Hideous, but valuable. From my research, I'd guess it's worth several thousand pounds. Items very similar to the one you described were made in the early twentieth century.'

'So,' I said, rubbing my chin in detective style, 'it would be well worth stealing. Which is unfortunate.'

'Why?' said Izzy. 'Are you thinking Heather really did steal it?'

'Absolutely definitely not!' I cried.

'Ooooh,' said Izzy, flashing her eyebrows up and down. 'I only asked! Could the great Saxby Smart be about to get a girlfriend?'

'Absolutely definitely not!' I cried again. I gave her a hard stare. 'As a matter of fact, I have a clear suspect, but I'm hoping I'm wrong on that score too. I need more proof, or a whole new theory to go on. What about the Mrs Pither insurance angle?'

'Well,' said Izzy, checking through her print-outs again, 'it's not easy to say for sure, but from various old newspaper cuttings I'd say that Mrs Pither was seriously rich.'

'Really? And she goes around in that tatty old coat. She must make Scrooge look like a money-wasting big spender!'

'I'm afraid it knocks your idea about an insurance scam on the head,' said Izzy.

'Yes,' I sighed. 'If she's well off, she'd have no need to pretend the clasp was lost in order to get hold of insurance money. Which points even more in the direction of a simple theft.'

"Fraid so,' said Izzy.

A further thought occurred to me. 'The thief would want to get rid of it quickly. The longer he left it, the more chance of being discovered with it.'

Izzy snapped her fingers. 'I'm one step ahead of you, as always! I've already checked all the internet sales and auction sites. Nothing.'

'He might well want to sell it on the quiet,' I said. 'Keep an eye on those websites, I'll check around town. Heeey, hang on, what d'you mean "as always" . . .?'

Once I got back home, I went through the phone book and made a list of all the local shops and dealers who might trade in jewellery. I spent the rest of the day trudging around the town centre, notebook in hand, asking at one place after another if they'd been offered anything like the clasp. Nobody had. I also asked if they knew of any other dealers who might be able to help me, who weren't already on my list. Nobody did.

At each shop, I used a cover story: I said that my dotty old aunt had given the clasp to a friend to sell for her by mistake. Honestly, she's soooo dotty, that aunt of mine! I said it was her *necklace* she meant to sell, and she was willing to buy the clasp back, if anyone had it. I needed to use a cover story because if any of the dealers *had* got the clasp, they might clam up if I started saying I was looking for something stolen. Or even if I said it was just plain lost – it could have been picked up in the street and sold by anyone.

My lack of success left me even more confused and worried than I'd been before. I retreated to my shed, and sat in my Thinking Chair, feet up on the desk, staring out of the shed window. It had started raining, yet again, and droplets were thumping against the shed's wooden roof. I made a few notes:

Reasons for Thinking that Tim Did It:

• **He had the opportunity.** Mrs Pither's coat, plus clasp, were hanging up in the hall all that time. He was at home. Nobody checked up on him during that time.

• **He has the motive.** He could definitely do with the money!

Evidence: He had that book with him. He was checking on prices, etc.

Reasons for Not Thinking that Tim Did It:

• The clasp hasn't been sold. If Tim needs the money, and doesn't want to be found out, he'd surely have sold it as soon as he could. It wouldn't make any sense NOT to sell it.
• In theory, Heather COULD still have done it. Although, she doesn't have the money motive for stealing the clasp that Tim does. Unless I'm missing something . . .

Whichever way I looked at it, I had a big problem. It was teatime on Saturday and Mrs Pither would be turning up at Heather's house to cause trouble on Monday morning. In the meantime, as the old joke goes, I was like a man with no toilet. I had nothing to go on.

What could I do to prove Tim's guilt? Or his innocence? If he still had the clasp – which seemed likely, since it hadn't been sold – then the only thing to do would be to go through his room! And there was no way I could do that. I couldn't march into Heather's house, accuse her brother of being a thief, and ransack his bedroom. Could I?

But, if I was *right*, I'd have revealed the culprit, with the dreadful side effect, in doing so, of causing a great deal of heartache for Heather's family.

But, if I accused him and was *wrong*, my reputation as a detective would be in tatters. And Tim wouldn't exactly be my greatest fan, either. (Besides, Tim could have hidden that clasp in any number of locations – it wouldn't have to be in his room. If that was the case, I'd be back to square one, *and* I'd have alerted him to my suspicions.)

Whether I was right or wrong, there was trouble ahead. I sat back in my Thinking Chair, wondering if there was something I'd not considered. Some little detail that would give me a few answers. Some fact about the events in Heather's house which would settle the question of Tim's involvement once and for all . . .

I almost leapt out of my Thinking Chair. Of course! There were three somethings which gave me the answer at last:

1. Something about the clasp itself.

2. Something about Mrs Pither's penny-pinching habits.

3. Something about Mrs Pither herself, that I'd noticed during my visit to Heather's house.

Tim *was* innocent. And so was Heather. I had the solution to the mystery!

Think back carefully . . .

CHAPTER SIX

MONDAY MORNING, NINE-THIRTY A.M. I was at Heather's house. (Teacher Training day!)

Tim was at the college, Heather was sitting nervously on the sofa in the living room, and Heather's mum was pacing about, from hall to kitchen to living room to hall and back again.

'Are you sure about this, Saxby?' she said, as she passed through the living room on her way back to the kitchen.

'I promise you, I'm never wrong,' I called after her. Her slippers slop-flopped up and down the hall.

'You'd better not be,' said Heather quietly. 'Because if you are, I'm in dead trouble in precisely . . .' She checked her watch. ' . . . twenty-eight minutes.'

'Relax,' I said. 'Got any more of those biccies?'

Twenty minutes later, a car drew up outside, and there was a ratt-ratt-ratt-ratt at the door. Heather pulled her legs up under her on the sofa and gulped. After a few seconds, Mrs Pither came swanning into the room and sat herself down in an armchair. I was pleased to see that she hadn't bothered to hang her ratty old green coat up in the hall. Heather's mum bustled in after her.

'Now then,' announced Mrs Pither. 'I want my clasp returned, immediately and undamaged. I'm a very generous and understanding person, so I'm prepared to involve the authorities only to the minimum extent in this case, provided my clasp is placed in my hands right now. And before you ask, no, I will not accept a cheque for its value. It is an heirloom. Its value is immaterial.'

Her baleful gaze swept across the room, like a leopard sizing up its prey. 'Well?' she barked.

'Eileen,' said Heather's mum, after a deep breath. 'We've been patient over this, because we realise it must be distressing to —'

'Are you claiming that you *don't* have my clasp?' cried Mrs Pither.

'Of course not!' cried Heather. 'We've been telling you that all along!'

Heather's mum held a hand out towards Heather, as if to say 'It's OK, don't lose your temper.'

'Saxby here says he knows what happened to your clasp,' said Heather's mum.

Mrs Pither looked at me. I shuddered. 'The boy with the ridiculous name?' she piped. 'You stole it?'

'No,' I said. 'But I can, as you put it, place it in your hands.'

'Then do so, you nasty little boy!'

'But first,' I said, being really, really calm, 'I think it's only fair if you apologise to Heather.'

'I *beg* your pardon?' piped Mrs Pither.

'Surely, if I can prove that Heather had nothing to do with the disappearance of your clasp, the least she deserves is an apology?'

Mrs Pither looked as if she'd just chewed up half a dozen hot chillis and was trying not to show it. I decided it was time for a full explanation.

'This case rests on a couple of small details. Details which might have been overlooked, if not for a third small detail. Like you, Mrs Pither, I assumed that the clasp had been stolen, because it was clearly nowhere to be found. At first, I thought the culprit was Tim, for various reasons we don't need to go into at the moment.

'However, once I'd worked out the truth, I could also guess what Tim was up to. He was doing exactly what I was doing, and investigating the matter. He was finding out about the clasp because he'd wondered, like I'd wondered, if Mrs Pither was trying to pull off some sort of insurance scam.'

'I *beg* your pardon?' repeated Mrs Pither.

'But I'm only making a guess there. I guess maybe Tim reached a dead end in his enquiries,' I continued, 'because he hasn't been around to notice these three details I mentioned.

'Detail number one: the clasp itself. Heather described it to me as having a big, sharp pin-type clip at the back. In other words, it's something that can give you a bit of a jab when it's undone.

'Detail number two: Mrs Pither's coat. Now, Mrs Pither is clearly a lady who is careful with her cash. Nothing wrong with that, of course. But that coat of hers has, if you'll pardon my saying so, seen better days.

'Detail number three: the other day, when I was here, Mrs Pither complained about her ankle. She said it had been bothering her, and she kept rubbing it. She thought it had been bitten by insects. She even made delicate, polite enquiries about whether that sofa there had fleas.

'There's nothing unusual about someone getting a few insect bites, is there? Except that it's hardly insect weather, is it? It's been wet, cold and miserable for days. And why only bite her on one ankle?

'Taking into account detail number one and detail number two, this third detail solved the puzzle for me. The clasp was not stolen. The clasp was not even lost, not strictly speaking. Why? Because, while the coat was hung up in the hall out there, the clasp dropped off. Perhaps Mrs Pither hadn't done it up correctly, it's impossible to say.

'It didn't fall on to the floor, or into the recycling box. It fell into the lining of Mrs Pither's old and tatty coat. That coat is frayed at the edges, and clearly threadbare. An object with a sharp point on it could easily get hooked on to something so well-worn. It didn't get hooked on the outside of the coat, or it would have been spotted. So it must have got hooked on the inside.

'And the clasp was, of course, still undone. Its point was sticking out, and poking through the material of the coat. We can even, er, "pinpoint" the clasp. Mrs Pither never goes anywhere without that coat, and as she walked the point of the clasp nicked her ankle. She thought she'd been bitten. Now, if I'm right, Mrs Pither, you've had the clasp yourself all along. Could you stand up, please, and raise the left hem of your coat?'

'I *beg* your pardon?' piped Mrs Pither. 'I've never heard such nonsense in all my life! As if I would be so careless as to leave a valuable clasp undone! As if I can't tell flea bites from the scratching of a pin!'

'If you could just go along with Saxby, for a moment?' said Heather's mum. 'We'll soon see if he's right or not.'

Mrs Pither snorted crossly, and stood up. She bent, took the hem of her coat between thumb and forefinger and lifted it up, so that its bottom edge was upside down.

Nothing.

'Give it a little shake,' I said.

She gave it a little shake.

Clunk!

The clasp hit the wooden floor, its pin wagging like a dog's tail. It was indeed an ugly piece of jewellery. Tiny gems glittered along the fingers of two silver hands, one gripped around the other.

Mrs Pither stood there, staring at it. Heather and her mum stifled their laughter. I cleared my throat.

'So, umm, Mrs Pither,' I said. 'Was there something you were going to say to Heather?'

Mrs Pither suddenly snatched the clasp off the floor and pocketed it. She glared at the three of us, stony-faced, as if we'd just caught her washing her undies in the sink. She looked at Heather.

'I . . .' There was quite a long pause. ' . . . Owe you an apology,' she barked at last.

She marched out of the room, and out of the house. Then she realised she'd organised her nephew to go to the post office in the car, and marched back inside while she phoned him.

Meanwhile, in the living room, Heather and her mum took it in turns to hug me. Tim returned home a little later, and Heather made him drop his sandwich in surprise when she asked him how his investigation was going.

I returned to my garden shed to make a few notes. I sat back in my Thinking Chair, my feet up on the desk, and felt pretty good about things in general.

Case closed.